LETTERS FROM AN
AMERICAN FARMER

SELECTIONS

LETTERS FROM AN AMERICAN FARMER

SELECTIONS

J. Hector St. John de Crèvecoeur

a *Broadview Anthology of American Literature* edition

General Editors, *The Broadview Anthology of American Literature*:

Derrick R. Spires, Cornell University
Rachel Greenwald Smith, Saint Louis University
Christina Roberts, Seattle University
Joseph Rezek, Boston University
Justine S. Murison, University of Illinois, Urbana-Champaign
Laura L. Mielke, University of Kansas
Christopher Looby, University of California, Los Angeles
Rodrigo Lazo, University of California, Irvine
Alisha Knight, Washington College
Hsuan L. Hsu, University of California, Davis
Michael Everton, Simon Fraser University
Christine Bold, University of Guelph

broadview press

BROADVIEW PRESS – www.broadviewpress.com
Peterborough, Ontario, Canada

Founded in 1985, Broadview Press remains a wholly independent publishing house. Broadview's focus is on academic publishing: our titles are accessible to university and college students as well as scholars and general readers. With over 800 titles in print, Broadview has become a leading international publisher in the humanities, with world-wide distribution. Broadview is committed to environmentally responsible publishing and fair business practices.

Library and Archives Canada Cataloguing in Publication

Title: Letters from an American farmer : selections / J. Hector St. John de Crèvecoeur ; general editors, Derrick R. Spires (Cornell University), [and eleven others].
Names: St. John de Crèvecoeur, J. Hector, 1735-1813, author. | Spires, Derrick Ramon, editor.
Description: Series statement: A Broadview anthology of American literature edition | Includes bibliographical references.
Identifiers: Canadiana (print) 20230162215 | Canadiana (ebook) 20230162223 | ISBN 9781554816361 (softcover) | ISBN 9781770489035 (PDF) | ISBN 9781460408353 (EPUB)
Subjects: LCSH: National characteristics, American—Early works to 1800. | LCSH: Farm life—United States—History—18th century—Early works to 1800. | LCSH: United States—Social life and customs—1775-1783—Early works to 1800. | LCSH: United States—Description and travel—Early works to 1800. | LCSH: Nantucket Island (Mass.)—Social life and customs—18th century—Early works to 1800.
Classification: LCC E163 .S73 2023 | DDC 973.3—dc23

Broadview Press handles its own distribution in North America:
PO Box 1243, Peterborough, Ontario K9J 7H5, Canada
555 Riverwalk Parkway, Tonawanda, NY 14150, USA
Tel: (705) 743-8990; Fax: (705) 743-8353
email: customerservice@broadviewpress.com

For all territories outside of North America, distribution is handled by Eurospan Group.

Broadview Press acknowledges the financial
support of the Government of Canada
for our publishing activities.

Canada

Developmental Editor: Don LePan
Cover Designer: Lisa Brawn
Typesetter: Alexandria Stuart

The Broadview Anthology of American Literature is a collaborative undertaking, with significant editorial contributions from the General Editors, from a wide range of other academics, and from Broadview's in-house editorial staff. The Crèvecoeur material was prepared with input from the General Editors and, at Broadview, from Helena Snopek, Jennifer McCue, Genevieve Kirk, and Don LePan. Dennis D. Moore of Florida State University reviewed the material and provided helpful comments and suggestions; his assistance is gratefully acknowledged. (Full responsibility for any errors or omissions, however, rests with the publisher.)

PRINTED IN CANADA

Contents

Introduction

J. Hector St. John de Crèvecoeur
1735 – 1813

At once intimately familiar with and yet in ways an outsider to American culture, French-born J. Hector St. John de Crèvecoeur earned renown in his life as an authority on Americanness, during the very years when the nation's political character was being challenged and defined. His *Letters from an American Farmer* (1782) vividly brought both the successes and the failures of American society to life for European audiences, and earned him a smaller but still substantial reputation in the country they depicted. Long interpreted as the literal thoughts of their creator, the *Letters*, written in the persona of Pennsylvania-born "Farmer James," have a complex reception history that has been shaped by changing tastes and political currents, and complicated by the fact that different and sometimes conflicting versions of the text were published during Crèvecoeur's lifetime. For over two centuries readers have struggled to reconcile the different sides of "Farmer James," who writes that America is "the most perfect society now existing in the world," but who concludes, upon witnessing the horrors of American slavery, that Americans "certainly are not that class of beings which we vainly think ourselves to be."

Born to members of the petty nobility in Normandy in 1735, Michel-Guillaume Jean de Crèvecoeur received an austere classical education under the tutorship of Catholic Jesuits in Caen, before moving to England in 1754 to live with distant relatives. He moved to French Canada the following year, after the untimely death of his English fiancée, and was employed by the French militia as a surveyor and map-maker during the French and Indian War. He became widely commended for his skills as a cartographer, but a battle wound and his subsequent disgrace after an undisclosed controversy led Crèvecoeur to again seek a different life. By late 1759 Crèvecoeur was making his way southwards to the British colonies, intent on making a living as an American farmer.

Though he did not settle immediately—spending approximately a decade working on an itinerant basis as a tradesperson and surveyor throughout New York, New England, and the Great Lakes region—by 1769 Crèvecoeur had become a British subject, had changed his name to James Hector St. John, and had purchased a large tract of land in Orange County, New York. It was shortly after his marriage to the Protestant Mehitable Tippett that Crèvecoeur began his work on a series of pieces reflecting upon the burgeoning American culture he now found himself a part of. When the American Revolution broke out in 1776, Crèvecoeur was conflicted; his wife's family were staunch Loyalists, but many of his other acquaintances supported the colonial rebels. Crèvecoeur himself decided to evade the conflict by heading back to France with his son in 1780, ostensibly with the aim of securing his children's inheritance—though he was hindered in his efforts by a few months' stint as British prisoner of war, on suspicion of being a Patriot spy.

Having eventually reached England, Crèvecoeur sought a publisher for his now-complete series of literary pieces in the popular eighteenth-century genre of epistolary writing. The collection aroused the interest of publisher Thomas Davies (a friend of Samuel Johnson), and *Letters from an American Farmer; Describing Certain Provincial Situations, Manners, and Customs, Not Generally Known; and Conveying Some Idea of the Late and Present Interior Circumstances of the British Colonies in North America* was printed in London in 1782. The letters are narrated by the self-described "humble American Planter" Farmer James—a farmer in Pennsylvania rather than New York—and addressed to a "Mr. F.B.," a refined Englishman who is described as having visited Farmer James and his wife on their homestead, and who is said to be still curious about the state of affairs in the colonies. They describe a good deal of the culture, industry, geography, and politics of early America—and convey too a good deal of emotional content, as Mr. F.B. is said in Letter 2 to have requested: "... you used, in your refined style, to denominate me the farmer of feelings. How rude must those feelings be in him who daily holds the ax or the plough! ... Those feelings, however, I will delineate as well as I can, agreeably to your earnest request."

With peace negotiations now well under way between Britain and the United States, Davies advertised the work as the unvarnished truth, asserting that the letters contained "much authentic information, little known on this side the Atlantic. They cannot, therefore, fail of being highly interesting, to the people of England, at a time when everybody's attention is directed toward the affairs of America." The collection was an immediate success in England. The *Letters*'s blend of sentimentality, romanticism, and Enlightenment political values rendered them highly interesting to a wide variety of audiences; a second edition was soon printed in London, and translations into Dutch and German ensued. Crèvecoeur's narrator both praises America as a farmer's paradise (and cultural melting pot) and condemns it as a place of horrendous enslavement and violent warfare, but many readers appeared to pay attention primarily to the more optimistic opening letters; indeed, the collection received some criticism on both sides of the Atlantic for what George Washington, otherwise an admirer of the work, described as a "too flattering" portrait of the nation.

Crèvecoeur soon returned to France, where he found himself a celebrity and began associating with members of the Parisian intellectual elite, while also working on a substantially altered French version of the *Lettres d'un Cultivateur Américain* (1784; 1787). Though he had appeared to harbor a degree of Loyalist sympathy while living in the rebelling colonies, here Crèvecoeur was embraced by the French as a specimen of an American Patriot, an image underscored by the intensely anti-British stance taken by many of the letters in the French-language edition. Largely abandoning the framing conceit of Farmer James, the French text provides a more explicitly philosophical exploration of Crèvecoeur's themes; the influence of French *philosophes* such as Rousseau and Voltaire is evident.

The growing tension between Crèvecoeur's French and American identities only increased when he was sent to the United States as a consul by the French government in 1783. Crèvecoeur's return to New York late that year was marked by tragedy: he found that his wife had been killed, his homestead destroyed in a raid, and that his two other children had barely escaped death themselves, and been taken in by strangers in Boston. After several politically successful but emotionally exhausting years working in the United States, Crèvecoeur eventually resigned from his French governmental position. He returned to France permanently in 1790.

The timing of his return was unfortunate. Once again, the pacifist Crèvecoeur was surrounded by political turmoil as the French

Revolution took hold; many of his acquaintances were executed or sent into exile during the Reign of Terror in 1793–94. Crèvecoeur himself fled Paris for Germany. Later in the decade he supported himself by writing agricultural pamphlets in Normandy. His last major work, *Voyage dans la Haute-Pennsylvanie et dans l'état de New-York* (1801), was virtually ignored upon publication; some found the work's philosophical ambitiousness to be at odds with their vision of the quaint, artless sentimentality of Farmer James. Crèvecoeur died of heart complications in 1813.

In the decades following his death, *Letters from an American Farmer* fell into obscurity, remaining out of print for many decades. Some nineteenth-century critics admired it as a quaint historical curiosity; the 1856 *Cyclopaedia of American Literature* describes the text as "pleasing and agreeable" but "all sentiment and susceptibility ... looking at homely American life in the Claude Lorraine glass of fanciful enthusiasm." New editions published in 1904 and 1912 signaled a revival of scholarly interest; still, the *Letters* were read primarily as interesting sociological documents rather than as literary works—although D.H. Lawrence in his 1923 *Studies in Classic American Literature* acknowledged Crèvecoeur as the emotional "prototype of the American." That year also saw the publication of *Sketches of Eighteenth Century America*, a collection of letters that had not made it into Crèvecoeur's original collection, though some of them had provided the basis for portions of the French *Lettres*.

It was only in the latter half of the twentieth century that literary scholars began to read the *Letters* with a view to their almost novelistic quality, acknowledging Crèvecoeur's Farmer James as a literary creation rather than as simply a version of his author, and taking into fuller consideration the thematic progression of the twelve letters considered as a whole. Interest among historians increased as well, as scholars came to see Crèvecoeur's influence on contemporary works such as Thomas Jefferson's *Notes on the State of Virginia* (1787), as well as on early sociological writings such as Alexis de Tocqueville's monumental *Democracy in America* (1835–40). In the twenty-first century scholarly interest has grown further, particularly in the wake of Dennis D. Moore's edition (2013), which brings together the twelve *Letters* with more than a dozen other essays by Crèvecoeur.

Note on the Text

The text presented in this edition is based on the two earliest London editions of *Letters from an American Farmer; Describing Certain Provincial Situations, Manners, and Customs, Not Generally Known; and Conveying Some Idea of the Late and Present Interior Circumstances of the British Colonies in North America* (1782 and 1783); the 1783 edition includes numerous corrections made by the author. Various modern editions—notably Dennis D. Moore's *Letters from an American Farmer and Other Essays* (2013)—have also been consulted. Spelling and punctuation have been modernized in accordance with the practices of *The Broadview Anthology of American Literature*. (An extended passage with the original spelling and punctuation preserved appears in the excerpt from Chapter 3.)

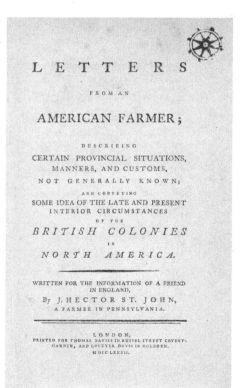

Letters from an American Farmer

Selections

from LETTER 2
ON THE SITUATION, FEELINGS, AND PLEASURES
OF AN AMERICAN FARMER

As you are the first enlightened European I have ever had the pleasure of being acquainted with, you will not be surprised that I should, according to your earnest desire and my promise, appear anxious of preserving your friendship and correspondence. By your accounts, I observe [that] a material difference subsists between your husbandry, modes, and customs, and ours. Everything is local. Could we enjoy the advantages of the English farmer, we should be much happier, indeed; but this wish, like many others, implies a contradiction; and could the English farmer have some of those privileges we possess, they would be the first[1] of their class in the world. Good and evil, I see, are to be found in all societies, and it is in vain to seek for any spot where those ingredients are not mixed. I therefore rest satisfied, and thank God that my lot is to be an American farmer, instead of a Russian boor, or a Hungarian peasant. I thank you kindly for the idea, however dreadful, which you have given me of their lot and condition; your observations have confirmed me in the justness of my ideas, and I am happier now than I thought myself before. It is strange that misery, when viewed in others, should become to us a sort of real good, though I am far from rejoicing to hear that there are in the world men so thoroughly wretched. They are no doubt as harmless, industrious, and willing to work as we are. Hard is their fate to be thus condemned to a slavery worse than that of our negroes. Yet, when young, I entertained some thoughts of selling my farm. I thought it afforded but a dull repetition of the same labours and pleasures. I thought the former tedious and heavy, the latter few and insipid. But when I came to consider myself as divested of my farm, I then found the world so wide, and every place so full, that I began to fear lest there would be no room for me. My farm, my house, my barn, presented to my imagination objects from which I adduced quite new ideas; they were more forcible than before. Why should not I find myself happy, said I, where my father was before? He left me no good books it is true; he gave me no other education than the art of

---

1 *first* Most well off.

reading and writing: but he left me a good farm, and his experience; he left me free from debts, and no kind of difficulties to struggle with. I married, and this perfectly reconciled me to my situation. My wife rendered my house all at once cheerful and pleasing; it no longer appeared gloomy and solitary as before. When I went to work in my fields, I worked with more alacrity and sprightliness. I felt that I did not work for myself alone, and this encouraged me much. My wife would often come with her knitting in her hand, and sit under the shady trees, praising the straightness of my furrows and the docility of my horses. This swelled my heart and made everything light and pleasant, and I regretted that I had not married before. I felt myself happy in my new situation, and where is that station which can confer a more substantial system of felicity than that of an American farmer, possessing freedom of action, freedom of thoughts, ruled by a mode of government which requires but little from us? I owe nothing but a peppercorn[1] to my country, a small tribute to my king, with loyalty and due respect. I know no other landlord than the Lord of all land, to whom I owe the most sincere gratitude. My father left me three hundred and seventy-one acres of land, forty-seven of which are good timothy[2] meadow, an excellent orchard, a good house, and a substantial barn. It is my duty to think how happy I am that he lived to build and to pay for all these improvements. What are the labours which I have to undergo? What are my fatigues, when compared to his, who had everything to do, from the first tree he felled to the finishing of his house? Every year I kill from 1,500 to 2,000 weight of pork, 1,200 of beef, half a dozen of good wethers[3] in harvest; of fowls my wife has always a great stock: what can I wish more? My negroes[4] are tolerably faithful and healthy. By a long series of industry and honest dealings, my father left behind him the name of a good man. I have but to

---

1   *peppercorn*   Small, insignificant amount (in this case, a small tithe or amount of tax).

2   *timothy*   Type of grass, commonly used to graze cattle and horses or to make hay.

3   *wethers*   Male sheep.

4   *My negroes*   Farmer James uses the expression "my negroes" again in Letter 12 when he makes this declaration: "I intend to say to my negroes—In the name of God, be free, my honest lads, I thank you for your past services; go, from henceforth, and work for yourselves; look on me as your old friend, and fellow labourer." In 1780, Pennsylvania (the state in which Farmer James resides) became the first state to begin to abolish slavery, though its gradual approach to emancipation meant that many people remained enslaved well into the 1800s.

tread his paths to be happy and a good man like him. I know enough of the law to regulate my little concerns with propriety, nor do I dread its power. These are the grand outlines of my situation; but as I can feel much more than I am able to express, I hardly know how to proceed. When my first son was born, the whole train of my ideas was suddenly altered. Never was there a charm that acted so quickly and powerfully. I ceased to ramble in imagination through the wide world. My excursions, since, have not exceeded the bounds of my farm, and all my principal pleasures are now centred within its scanty limits: but, at the same time, there is not an operation belonging to it in which I do not find some food for useful reflections. This is the reason, I suppose, that when you were here, you used, in your refined style, to denominate me the farmer of feelings. How rude[1] must those feelings be in him who daily holds the ax or the plough! How much more refined, on the contrary, those of the European, whose mind is improved by education, example, books, and by every acquired advantage! Those feelings, however, I will delineate as well as I can, agreeably to your earnest request. When I contemplate my wife, by my fireside, while she either spins, knits, darns, or suckles our child, I cannot describe the various emotions of love, of gratitude, of conscious pride, which thrill in my heart, and often overflow in involuntary tears. I feel the necessity, the sweet pleasure, of acting my part, the part of an husband and father, with an attention and propriety which may entitle me to my good fortune. It is true these pleasing images vanish with the smoke of my pipe, but, though they disappear from my mind, the impression they have made on my heart is indelible. When I play with the infant, my warm imagination runs forward, and eagerly anticipates his future temper and constitution. I would willingly open the book of fate, and know in which page his destiny is delineated. Alas! where is the father who, in those moments of paternal ecstasy, can delineate one half of the thoughts which dilate his heart? I am sure I cannot. Then again I fear for the health of those who are become so dear to me, and, in their sicknesses, I severely pay for the joys I experienced while they were well. Whenever I go abroad it is always involuntary. I never return home without feeling some pleasing emotion, which I often suppress as useless and foolish. The

---

1 *rude* Uncultivated.

instant I enter on my own land, the bright idea of property, of exclusive right, of independence, exalt my mind. Precious soil, I say to myself, by what singular custom of law is it that thou wast made to constitute the riches of the freeholder? What should we American farmers be without the distinct possession of that soil? It feeds, it clothes us; from it we draw even a great exuberancy, our best meat, our richest drink; the very honey of our bees comes from this privileged spot. No wonder we should thus cherish its possession; no wonder that so many Europeans, who have never been able to say that such portion of land was theirs, cross the Atlantic to realize that happiness! This formerly rude soil has been converted by my father into a pleasant farm, and, in return it has established all our rights. On it is founded our rank, our freedom, our power as citizens; our importance as inhabitants of such a district. These images, I must confess, I always behold with pleasure, and extend them as far as my imagination can reach: for this is what may be called the true and the only philosophy of an American farmer. Pray do not laugh in thus seeing an artless countryman tracing himself through the simple modifications of his life. Remember that you have required it, therefore, with candor, though with diffidence, I endeavour to follow the thread of my feelings, but I cannot tell you all. Often, when I plough my low ground, I place my little boy on a chair which screws to the beam of the plough. Its motion and that of the horses please him; he is perfectly happy, and begins to chat. As I lean over the handle, various are the thoughts which crowd into my mind. I am now doing for him, I say, what my father formerly did for me; may God enable him to live that he may perform the same operations for the same purposes when I am worn out and old! I relieve his mother of some trouble while I have him with me; the odoriferous furrow exhilarates his spirits, and seems to do the child a great deal of good, for he looks more blooming since I have adopted that practice. Can more pleasure, more dignity, be added to that primary occupation? The father, thus ploughing with his child, and to feed his family, is inferior only to the emperor of China ploughing as an example to his kingdom. In the evening, when I return home through my low grounds, I am astonished at the myriads of insects which I perceive dancing in the beams of the setting sun. I was before scarcely acquainted with their existence; they are so small that it is difficult to distinguish them; they are carefully improving this short evening space, not daring to expose themselves to the blaze of our meridian sun. I never see an egg brought on my table but I feel penetrated with the wonderful change it would have undergone but for my gluttony. It might have been a gentle useful hen leading her chickens with a care and vigilance which speaks shame to many women. A cock, perhaps, arrayed with the most majestic plumes, tender to its mate, bold, courageous, endowed with an astonishing instinct, with thoughts, with memory, and every distinguishing characteristic of the reason of man! I never see my trees drop their leaves and their fruit in the autumn, and bud again in the spring, without wonder. The sagacity of those animals, which have long been the tenants of my farm, astonish me: some of them seem to surpass even men in memory and sagacity. I could tell you singular instances of that kind. What then is this instinct which we so debase, and of which we are taught to entertain so diminutive an idea? My bees, above any other tenants of my farm, attract my attention and respect. I am astonished to see that nothing exists but what has its enemy; one species pursue and live upon the other. Unfortunately, our kingbirds are the destroyers of those industrious insects; but, on the other hand, these birds preserve our fields from the depredation of crows which they pursue on the wing with great vigilance and astonishing dexterity. Thus divided by two interested motives, I have long resisted the desire I had to kill them, until last year, when I thought they[1] increased too much, and my indulgence had been carried too far. It was at the time of swarming, when they all came and fixed themselves on the neighbouring trees, whence they caught those that returned loaded from the fields.[2] This made me resolve to kill as many as I could, and I was just ready to fire, when a bunch of bees as big as my fist issued from one of the hives, rushed on one of the birds, and probably stung him, for he instantly screamed, and flew, not as before in an irregular manner, but in a direct line. He was followed by the same bold phalanx,[3] at a considerable distance, which unfortunately becoming too sure of victory, quitted their military array and disbanded themselves. By this inconsiderate step they lost all that aggregate of force which had made the bird fly off. Perceiving their

---

1 *they* I.e., the kingbirds.
2 *those ... fields* I.e., the bees.
3 *phalanx* Small, compact body of soldiers.

disorder, he immediately returned and snapped as many as he wanted; nay, he had even the impudence to alight on the very twig from which the bees had driven him. I killed him and immediately opened his craw, from which I took 171 bees. I laid them all on a blanket in the sun, and, to my great surprise, 54 returned to life, licked themselves clean, and joyfully went back to the hive, where they probably informed their companions of such an adventure and escape as I believe had never happened before to American bees! I draw a great fund of pleasure from the quails which inhabit my farm; they abundantly repay me, by their various notes and peculiar tameness, for the inviolable hospitality I constantly show them in the winter. Instead of perfidiously taking advantage of their great and affecting distress, when nature offers nothing but a barren universal bed of snow, when irresistible necessity forces them to my barn doors, I permit them to feed unmolested; and it is not the least agreeable spectacle which that dreary season presents, when I see those beautiful birds, tamed by hunger, intermingling with all my cattle and sheep, seeking in security for the poor scanty grain which but for them would be useless and lost. Often, in the angles of the fences, where the motion of the wind prevents the snow from settling, I carry them both chaff[1] and grain; the one to feed them, the other to prevent their tender feet from freezing fast to the earth, as I have frequently observed them to do. I do not know an instance in which the singular barbarity of man is so strongly delineated, as in the catching and murdering those harmless birds, at that cruel season of the year. ...

from LETTER 3
WHAT IS AN AMERICAN?

I wish I could be acquainted with the feelings and thoughts which must agitate the heart and present themselves to the mind of an enlightened Englishman when he first lands on this continent. He must greatly rejoice that he lived at a time to see this fair country discovered and settled; he must necessarily feel a share of national pride, when he views the chain of settlements which embellishes these extended shores. When he says to himself, "This is the work of my

---

1   *chaff* Husks of grains or of corn.

countrymen, who, when convulsed by factions,[1] afflicted by a variety of miseries and wants, restless and impatient, took refuge here. They brought along with them their national genius,[2] to which they principally owe what liberty they enjoy, and what substance they possess." Here he sees the industry of his native country displayed in a new manner, and traces in their works the embryos of all the arts, sciences, and ingenuity which flourish in Europe. Here he beholds fair cities, substantial villages, extensive fields, an immense country filled with decent houses, good roads, orchards, meadows, and bridges, where an hundred years ago all was wild, woody and uncultivated! What a train of pleasing ideas this fair spectacle must suggest; it is a prospect which must inspire a good citizen with the most heartfelt pleasure. The difficulty consists in the manner of viewing so extensive a scene. He is arrived on a new continent; a modern society offers itself to his contemplation, different from what he had hitherto seen. It is not composed, as in Europe, of great lords who possess everything, and of a herd of people who have nothing. Here are no aristocratical families, no courts, no kings, no bishops, no ecclesiastical dominion, no invisible power giving to a few a very visible one; no great manufacturers employing thousands, no great refinements of luxury. The rich and the poor are not so far removed from each other as they are in Europe. Some few towns excepted, we are all tillers of the earth, from Nova Scotia to West Florida. We are a people of cultivators, scattered over an immense territory, communicating with each other by means of good roads and navigable rivers, united by the silken bands of mild government, all respecting the laws, without dreading their power, because they are equitable. We are all animated with the spirit of an industry which is unfettered and unrestrained, because each person works for himself. If he travels through our rural districts he views not the hostile castle, and the haughty mansion, contrasted with the clay-built hut and miserable cabin, where cattle and men help to keep each other warm, and dwell in meanness, smoke, and indigence.[3] A pleasing uniformity of decent competence appears throughout our habitations. The meanest of our log-houses is a dry and comfortable habitation. Lawyer or merchant are the fairest titles our towns afford;

---

1   *convulsed by factions*   I.e., distressed or agitated by disputes.
2   *national genius*   I.e., the distinctive spirit and qualities of their respective nations.
3   *meanness*   Shabbiness or squalor; *indigence*   Poverty.

that of a farmer is the only appellation of the rural inhabitants of our country. It must take some time ere he can reconcile himself to our dictionary, which is but short in words of dignity, and names of honour. There, on a Sunday, he sees a congregation of respectable farmers and their wives, all clad in neat homespun,[1] well mounted, or riding in their own humble wagons. There is not among them an esquire, saving the unlettered[2] magistrate. There he sees a parson as simple as his flock, a farmer who does not riot[3] on the labour of others. We have no princes for whom we toil, starve, and bleed; we are the most perfect society now existing in the world. Here man is free as he ought to be; nor is this pleasing equality so transitory as many others are. Many ages will not see the shores of our great lakes replenished with inland nations, nor the unknown bounds of North America entirely peopled. Who can tell how far it extends? Who can tell the millions of men whom it will feed and contain? For no European foot has as yet travelled half the extent of this mighty continent!

The next wish of this traveller will be to know whence came all these people. They are a mixture of English, Scotch, Irish, French, Dutch, Germans, and Swedes. From this promiscuous[4] breed, that race now called Americans have arisen. The eastern provinces[5] must indeed be excepted, as being the unmixed descendants of Englishmen. I have heard many wish that they had been more intermixed also: for my part, I am no wisher, and think it much better as it has happened. They exhibit a most conspicuous figure in this great and variegated picture; they too enter for a great share in the pleasing perspective displayed in these thirteen provinces. I know it is fashionable to reflect on[6] them, but I respect them for what they have done; for the accuracy and wisdom with which they have settled their territory; for the decency of their manners; for their early love of letters;[7] their ancient college,[8] the first in this hemisphere; for their industry,[9] which

---

1 *homespun*   Clothing made from yarn or thread spun at home.
2 *saving*   Except for; *unlettered*   Unsophisticated; having a limited education.
3 *riot*   Make merry; live indulgently.
4 *promiscuous*   Varied; mixed.
5 *eastern provinces*   I.e., New England.
6 *reflect on*   Criticize or portray negatively.
7 *letters*   Learning.
8 *ancient college*   Harvard College in Massachusetts, established in 1636.
9 *industry*   Industriousness.

to me who am but a farmer, is the criterion of everything. There never was a people, situated as they are, who with so ungrateful a soil have done more in so short a time. Do you think that the monarchical ingredients, which are more prevalent in other governments, have purged them from all foul stains? Their histories assert the contrary.

In this great American asylum,[1] the poor of Europe have by some means met together, and in consequence of various causes; to what purpose should they ask one another what countrymen they are? Alas, two thirds of them had no country. Can a wretch who wanders about, who works and starves, whose life is a continual scene of sore affliction or pinching penury;[2] can that man call England or any other kingdom his country? A country that had no bread for him, whose fields procured him no harvest, who met with nothing but the frowns of the rich, the severity of the laws, with jails and punishments; who owned not a single foot of the extensive surface of this planet? No! urged by a variety of motives, here they came. Everything has tended to regenerate them: new laws, a new mode of living, a new social system. Here they are become men; in Europe they were as so many useless plants, wanting vegetative mould,[3] and refreshing showers. They withered, and were mowed down by want, hunger, and war; but now by the power of transplantation, like all other plants they have taken root and flourished! Formerly they were not numbered in any civil lists[4] of their country, except in those of the poor; here they rank as citizens. By what invisible power has this surprising metamorphosis been performed? By that of the laws and that of their industry. The laws, the indulgent[5] laws, protect them as they arrive, stamping on them the symbol of adoption; they receive ample rewards for their labours; these accumulated rewards procure them lands; those lands confer on them the title of freemen, and to that title every benefit is affixed which men can possibly require. This is the great operation daily performed by our laws. From whence proceed these laws? From our government. Whence the government? It is derived from the original genius and strong desire of the people ratified and confirmed

---

1 *asylum* Place of shelter or sanctuary.
2 *pinching penury* Biting poverty.
3 *wanting vegetative mould* I.e., lacking fertilizer.
4 *civil lists* Government records of significant members of a society.
5 *indulgent* Tolerant.

by the crown. This is the great chain which links us all, this is the picture which every province exhibits, Nova Scotia excepted.[1] There the crown has done all; either there were no people who had genius, or it was not much attended to: the consequence is, that the province is very thinly inhabited indeed; the power of the crown in conjunction with the musketos[2] has prevented men from settling there. Yet some parts of it flourished once, and it contained a mild, harmless set of people. But for the fault of a few leaders, the whole were banished. The greatest political error the crown ever committed in America, was to cut off men from a country which wanted nothing but men!

What attachment can a poor European emigrant have for a country where he had nothing? The knowledge of the language, the love of a few kindred as poor as himself, were the only cords that tied him: his country is now that which gives him land, bread, protection, and consequence; *Ubi panis ibi patria*,[3] is the motto of all emigrants. What then is the American, this new man? He is either an European, or the descendant of an European, hence that strange mixture of blood, which you will find in no other country. I could point out to you a family whose grandfather was an Englishman, whose wife was Dutch, whose son married a French woman, and whose present four sons have now four wives of different nations. *He* is an American, who leaving behind him all his ancient prejudices and manners, receives new ones from the new mode of life he has embraced, the new government he obeys, and the new rank he holds. He becomes an American by being received in the broad lap of our great *Alma Mater*.[4] Here individuals of all nations are melted into a new race of men, whose labours and posterity will one day cause great changes in the world. Americans are the western pilgrims, who are carrying along with them that great mass of arts, sciences, vigour, and industry which began long since in the east; they will finish the great circle. The Americans were once scattered all over Europe; here they are

---

1   *Nova Scotia excepted*   Reference to the 1755 Expulsion of the Acadians, which occurred in the wake of the French and Indian War, when longtime French Acadian settlers were forcibly removed from Nova Scotia by the British government for refusing to sign an oath of allegiance.

2   *musketos*   Mosquitos.

3   *Ubi panis ibi patria*   Latin: Where there is bread, there is my homeland.

4   *Alma Mater*   Latin: Bountiful Mother.

incorporated into one of the finest systems of population which has ever appeared, and which will hereafter become distinct by the power of the different climates they inhabit. The American ought therefore to love this country much better than that wherein either he or his forefathers were born. Here the rewards of his industry follow with equal steps the progress of his labour; his labour is founded on the basis of nature, *self-interest*; can it want a stronger allurement? Wives and children, who before in vain demanded of him a morsel of bread, now, fat and frolicksome, gladly help their father to clear those fields whence exuberant crops are to arise to feed and to clothe them all; without any part being claimed, either by a despotic prince, a rich abbot, or a mighty lord. Here religion demands but little of him; a small voluntary salary to the minister,[1] and gratitude to God; can he refuse these? The American is a new man, who acts upon new principles; he must therefore entertain new ideas, and form new opinions. From involuntary idleness, servile dependence, penury, and useless labour, he has passed to toils of a very different nature, rewarded by ample subsistence. This is an American.

British America is divided into many provinces, forming a large association, scattered along a coast 1,500 miles extent and about 200 wide. This society I would fain examine, at least such as it appears in the middle provinces; if it does not afford that variety of tinges and gradations which may be observed in Europe, we have colours peculiar to ourselves. For instance, it is natural to conceive that those who live near the sea must be very different from those who live in the woods; the intermediate space will afford a separate and distinct class.

Men are like plants; the goodness and flavour of the fruit proceeds from the peculiar soil and exposition in which they grow. We are nothing but what we derive from the air we breathe, the climate we inhabit, the government we obey, the system of religion we profess, and the nature of our employment. Here you will find but few crimes; these have acquired as yet no root among us. I wish I were able to trace all my ideas; if my ignorance prevents me from describing them properly, I hope I shall be able to delineate a few of the outlines, which are all I propose.

---

1   *voluntary ... minister* In parts of Europe, payment of tithes to the established church—which funded the salaries of the clergy—was compulsory, even for those who did not belong to the established church.

Those who live near the sea, feed more on fish than on flesh, and often encounter that boisterous element. This renders them more bold and enterprising; this leads them to neglect the confined occupations of the land. They see and converse with a variety of people; their intercourse[1] with mankind becomes extensive. The sea inspires them with a love of traffic,[2] a desire of transporting produce from one place to another; and leads them to a variety of resources which supply the place of labour. Those who inhabit the middle settlements, by far the most numerous, must be very different; the simple cultivation of the earth purifies them, but the indulgences of the government, the soft remonstrances of religion, the rank of independent freeholders,[3] must necessarily inspire them with sentiments very little known in Europe among people of the same class. What do I say? Europe has no such class of men; the early knowledge they acquire, the early bargains they make, give them a great degree of sagacity. As freemen they will be litigious; pride and obstinacy are often the cause of lawsuits; the nature of our laws and governments may be another. As citizens it is easy to imagine that they will carefully read the newspapers, enter into every political disquisition, freely blame or censure governors and others. As farmers they will be careful and anxious to get as much as they can, because what they get is their own. As northern men they will love the cheerful cup. As Christians, religion curbs them not in their opinions; the general indulgence leaves everyone to think for themselves in spiritual matters; the laws inspect our actions, our thoughts are left to God. Industry, good living, selfishness, litigiousness, country politics, the pride of freemen, religious indifference, are their characteristics. If you recede still farther from the sea, you will come into more modern settlements; they exhibit the same strong lineaments, in a ruder[4] appearance. Religion seems to have still less influence, and their manners are less improved.

Now we arrive near the great woods, near the last inhabited districts;[5] there men seem to be placed still farther beyond the reach

---

1 *intercourse* Interactions.
2 *traffic* Trade.
3 *freeholders* Landowners.
4 *ruder* Less refined.
5 *last inhabited districts* I.e., the "frontier" regions beyond the borders of the Thirteen Colonies.

of government, which in some measure leaves them to themselves. How can it pervade every corner? As they were driven there by misfortunes, necessity of beginnings, desire of acquiring large tracks of land, idleness, frequent want of economy,[1] ancient debts; the reunion of such people does not afford a very pleasing spectacle. When discord, want of unity and friendship; when either drunkenness or idleness prevail in such remote districts, contention, inactivity, and wretchedness must ensue. There are not the same remedies to these evils as in a long-established community. The few magistrates they have are in general little better than the rest; they are often in a perfect state of war; that of man against man, sometimes decided by blows, sometimes by means of the law; that of man against every wild inhabitant of these venerable woods, of which they are come to dispossess them. There men appear to be no better than carnivorous animals of a superior rank, living on the flesh of wild animals when they can catch them, and when they are not able, they subsist on grain. He who would wish to see America in its proper light, and have a true idea of its feeble beginnings and barbarous rudiments, must visit our extended line of frontiers where the last settlers dwell, and where he may see the first labours of settlement, the mode of clearing the earth, in their different appearances; where men are wholly left dependent on their native tempers, and on the spur of uncertain industry, which often fails when not sanctified by the efficacy of a few moral rules. There, remote from the power of example, and check of shame,[2] many families exhibit the most hideous parts of our society. They are a kind of forlorn hope, preceding by ten or twelve years the most respectable army of veterans[3] which come after them. In that space, prosperity will polish some, vice and the law will drive off the rest, who uniting again with others like themselves will recede still farther; making room for more industrious people, who will finish their improvements, convert the log house into a convenient habitation, and rejoicing that the first heavy labours are finished, will change in a few years that hitherto barbarous country into a fine, fertile, well-regulated district. Such is our progress, such is the march of the Europeans toward the interior parts of this continent. In all

---

1 *want of economy* Poor management of personal finances.
2 *check of shame* I.e., the power of shame to change or restrain one's behavior.
3 *veterans* Experienced settlers.

societies there are off-casts; this impure part serves as our precursors or pioneers; my father himself was one of that class,[1] but he came upon honest principles, and was therefore one of the few who held fast; by good conduct and temperance he transmitted to me his fair inheritance, when not above one in fourteen of his contemporaries had the same good fortune.

Forty years ago this smiling country was thus inhabited; it is now purged, a general decency of manners prevails throughout, and such has been the fate of our best countries.

Exclusive of those general characteristics, each province has its own, founded on the government, climate, mode of husbandry,[2] customs, and peculiarity of circumstances. Europeans submit insensibly to these great powers, and become, in the course of a few generations, not only Americans in general, but either Pennsylvanians, Virginians, or provincials under some other name. Whoever traverses the continent must easily observe those strong differences, which will grow more evident in time. The inhabitants of Canada, Massachusetts, the middle provinces, the southern ones will be as different as their climates; their only points of unity will be those of religion and language.

As I have endeavoured to show you how Europeans become Americans, it may not be disagreeable to show you likewise how the various Christian sects introduced wear out, and how religious indifference becomes prevalent. When any considerable number of a particular sect happen to dwell contiguous to each other, they immediately erect a temple, and there worship the Divinity agreeably to their own peculiar ideas. Nobody disturbs them. If any new sect springs up in Europe, it may happen that many of its professors[3] will come and settle in America. As they bring their zeal with them, they are at liberty to make proselytes if they can, and to build a meeting and to follow the dictates of their consciences; for neither the government nor any other power interferes. If they are peaceable subjects, and are industrious, what is it to their neighbours how and in what manner they think fit to address their prayers to the Supreme Being?

---

1   *my father ... that class*   Crèvecoeur's own father was a country gentleman in France who never visited America.
2   *husbandry*   Farming.
3   *professors*   Followers.

But if the sectaries are not settled close together, if they are mixed with other denominations, their zeal will cool for want of fuel, and will be extinguished in a little time. Then the Americans become as to religion, what they are as to country, allied to all. In them the name of Englishman, Frenchman, and European is lost, and in like manner, the strict modes of Christianity as practised in Europe are lost also. This effect will extend itself still farther hereafter, and though this may appear to you as a strange idea, yet it is a very true one. I shall be able perhaps hereafter to explain myself better; in the meanwhile, let the following example serve as my first justification.

Let us suppose you and I to be travelling. We observe that in this house, to the right, lives a Catholic, who prays to God as he has been taught, and believes in transubstantiation;[1] he works and raises wheat, he has a large family of children, all hale and robust; his belief, his prayers offend nobody. About one mile farther on the same road, his next neighbour may be a good honest plodding German Lutheran, who addresses himself to the same God, the God of all, agreeably to the modes he has been educated in, and believes in consubstantiation;[2] by so doing he scandalizes nobody; he also works in his fields, embellishes the earth, clears swamps, etc. What has the world to do with his Lutheran principles? He persecutes nobody, and nobody persecutes him; he visits his neighbours, and his neighbours visit him. Next to him lives a seceder,[3] the most enthusiastic of all sectaries; his zeal is hot and fiery, but separated as he is from others of the same complexion, he has no congregation of his own to resort to, where he might cabal[4] and mingle religious pride with worldly obstinacy. He likewise raises good crops, his house is handsomely painted, his orchard is one of the fairest in the neighbourhood. How does it concern the welfare of the country, or of the province at large, what this man's religious sentiments are, or really whether he has any at all? He is a good farmer, he is a sober, peaceable, good citizen. ...

---

1   *transubstantiation*   Central belief of Catholicism, that the bread and wine consumed during the ritual of the Eucharist literally transform into the body and blood of Christ.

2   *consubstantiation*   As opposed to transubstantiation, this doctrine holds that the bread and wine taken at communion represent the spiritual presence of Christ, but are not actually transformed into his body and blood.

3   *seceder*   One who has withdrawn participation from any formal religious organization.

4   *cabal*   Conspire with others; mingle dangerously.

This is the visible character; the invisible one is only guessed at, and is nobody's business. ... Each of these people instruct their children as well as they can, but these instructions are feeble compared to those which are given to the youth of the poorest class in Europe. Their children will therefore grow up less zealous and more indifferent in matters of religion than their parents. The foolish vanity, or rather the fury of making proselytes, is unknown here; they have no time, the seasons call for all their attention, and thus in a few years, this mixed neighbourhood will exhibit a strange religious medley, that will be neither pure Catholicism nor pure Calvinism.[1] A very perceptible indifference, even in the first generation, will become apparent; and it may happen that the daughter of the Catholic will marry the son of the seceder, and settle by themselves at a distance from their parents. What religious education will they give their children? A very imperfect one. If there happens to be in the neighbourhood any place of worship—we will suppose a Quaker's meeting—rather than not show their fine clothes,[2] they will go to it, and some of them may perhaps attach themselves to that society. Others will remain in a perfect state of indifference; the children of these zealous parents will not be able to tell what their religious principles are, and their grandchildren still less. ... Thus all sects are mixed as well as all nations; thus religious indifference is imperceptibly disseminated from one end of the continent to the other; which is at present one of the strongest characteristics of the Americans. Where this will reach no one can tell; perhaps it may leave a vacuum fit to receive other systems. Persecution, religious pride, the love of contradiction, are the food of what the world commonly calls religion. These motives have ceased here. Zeal in Europe is confined; here it evaporates in the great distance it has to travel. There it is a grain of powder enclosed;[3] here it burns away in the open air, and consumes without effect.

But to return to our back settlers. I must tell you that there is something in the proximity of the woods which is very singular. It is with men as it is with the plants and animals that grow and live in the

---

1 *Calvinism* Branch of Protestant belief based on the teachings of French dissenter John Calvin (1509–64), presented here as diametrically opposed to Catholicism.
2 *Quaker's meeting ... fine clothes* Quakers were known for their adherence to principles of plain dress.
3 *powder enclosed* I.e., as gunpowder is enclosed in a gun.

forests; they are entirely different from those that live in the plains. I will candidly tell you all my thoughts, but you are not to expect that I shall advance any reasons. By living in or near the woods, their actions are regulated by the wildness of the neighbourhood. The deer often come to eat their grain, the wolves to destroy their sheep, the bears to kill their hogs, the foxes to catch their poultry. This surrounding hostility immediately puts the gun into their hands; they watch these animals, they kill some; and thus by defending their property, they soon become professed hunters; this is the progress; once hunters, farewell to the plough. The chase renders them ferocious, gloomy, and unsociable; a hunter wants no neighbour, he rather hates them, because he dreads the competition. In a little time their success in the woods makes them neglect their tillage. They trust to the natural fecundity of the earth, and therefore do little; carelessness in fencing often exposes what little they sow to destruction; they are not at home to watch; in order therefore to make up the deficiency, they go oftener to the woods. That new mode of life brings along with it a new set of manners, which I cannot easily describe. These new manners, being grafted on the old stock, produce a strange sort of lawless profligacy, the impressions of which are indelible. The manners of the Indian natives are respectable, compared with this European medley. Their wives and children live in sloth and inactivity; and having no proper pursuits, you may judge what education the latter receive. Their tender minds have nothing else to contemplate but the example of their parents; like them they grow up a mongrel breed, half civilized, half savage, except nature stamps on them some constitutional propensities. That rich, that voluptuous sentiment is gone which struck them so forcibly; the possession of their freeholds no longer conveys to their minds the same pleasure and pride. To all these reasons you must add, their lonely[1] situation, and you cannot imagine what an effect on manners the great distances they live from each other has! Consider one of the last settlements in its first view: of what is it composed? Europeans who have not that sufficient share of knowledge they ought to have, in order to prosper; people who have suddenly passed from oppression, dread of government, and fear of laws, into the unlimited freedom of the woods. This sudden

---

1 *lonely* I.e., remote and unpopulated.

change must have a very great effect on most men, and on that class particularly. Eating of wild meat, whatever you may think, tends to alter their temper; though all the proof I can adduce is that I have seen it: and having no place of worship to resort to, what little society this might afford is denied them. ... Thus our bad people are those who are half cultivators and half hunters; and the worst of them are those who have degenerated altogether into the hunting state. As old ploughmen and new men of the woods, as Europeans and new-made Indians, they contract the vices of both; they adopt the moroseness and ferocity of a native, without his mildness, or even his industry at home. If manners are not refined, at least they are rendered simple and inoffensive by tilling the earth; all our wants are supplied by it, our time is divided between labour and rest, and leaves none for the commission of great misdeeds. As hunters it is divided between the toil of the chase, the idleness of repose, or the indulgence of inebriation. Hunting is but a licentious idle life, and if it does not always pervert good dispositions; yet, when it is united with bad luck, it leads to want: want stimulates that propensity to rapacity and injustice, too natural to needy men, which is the fatal gradation. After this explanation of the effects which follow by living in the woods, shall we yet vainly flatter ourselves with the hope of converting the Indians? We should rather begin with converting our back-settlers; and now if I dare mention the name of religion, its sweet accents would be lost in the immensity of these woods. Men thus placed, are not fit either to receive or remember its mild instructions; they want temples and ministers, but as soon as men cease to remain at home, and begin to lead an erratic life, let them be either tawny or white, they cease to be its disciples. ...

Europe contains hardly any other distinctions but lords and tenants; this fair country alone is settled by freeholders, the possessors of the soil they cultivate, members of the government they obey, and the framers of their own laws, by means of their representatives. This is a thought which you have taught me to cherish; our distance from Europe, far from diminishing, rather adds to our usefulness and consequence as men and subjects. Had our forefathers remained there, they would only have crouded it, and perhaps prolonged those convulsions which had shook it so long. Every industrious European who transports himself here, may be compared to a sprout growing

original spelling

at the foot of a great tree; it enjoys and draws but a little portion of sap; wrench it from the parent roots, transplant it, and it will become a tree bearing fruit also. Colonists are therefore intitled to the consideration due to the most useful subjects; a hundred families barely existing in some parts of Scotland, will here in six years, case an annual exportation of 10,000 bushels of wheat: 100 bushels being but a common quantity for an industrious family to sell, if they cultivate good land. It is here then that the idle may be employed, the useless become useful, and the poor become rich; but by riches I do not mean gold and silver, we have but little of those metals; I mean a better sort of wealth, cleared lands, cattle, good houses, good cloaths, and an increase of people to enjoy them.

There is no wonder that this country has so many charms, and presents to Europeans so many temptations to remain in it. A traveller in Europe becomes a stranger as soon as he quits his own kingdom; but it is otherwise here. We know, properly speaking, no strangers; this is every person's country; the variety of our soils, situations, climates, governments, and produce, hath something which must please every body. No sooner does an European arrive, no matter of what condition, than his eyes are opened upon the fair prospect; he hears his language spoke, he retraces many of his own country manners, he perpetually hears the names of families and towns with which he is acquainted; he sees happiness and prosperity in all places disseminated; he meets with hospitality, kindness, and plenty every where; he beholds hardly any poor, he seldom hears of punishments and executions; and he wonders at the elegance of our towns, those miracles of industry and freedom. He cannot admire enough our rural districts, our convenient roads, good taverns, and our many accommodations; he involuntarily loves a country where every thing is so lovely. When in England, he was a mere Englishman; here he stands on a larger portion of the globe, not less than its fourth part, and may see the productions of the north, in iron and naval stores; the provisions of Ireland, the grain of Egypt, the indigo, the rice of China. He does not find, as in Europe, a crouded society, where every place is over-stocked; he does not feel that perpetual collision of parties, that difficulty of beginning, that contention which oversets so many. There is room for every body in America; has he any particular talent, or industry? he exerts it in order to procure a livelihood, and

original spelling

it succeeds. Is he a merchant? the avenues of trade are infinite; is he eminent in any respect? he will be employed and respected. Does he love a country life? pleasant farms present themselves; he may purchase what he wants, and thereby become an American farmer. Is he a labourer, sober and industrious? he need not go many miles, nor receive many informations before he will be hired, well fed at the table of his employer, and paid four or five times more than he can get in Europe. Does he want uncultivated lands? thousands of acres present themselves, which he may purchase cheap. Whatever be his talents or inclinations, if they are moderate, he may satisfy them. I do not mean that every one who comes will grow rich in a little time; no, but he may procure an easy, decent maintenance, by his industry. Instead of starving he will be fed, instead of being idle he will have employment; and these are riches enough for such men as come over here. The rich stay in Europe, it is only the middling and poor that emigrate. Would you wish to travel in independent idleness, from north to south, you will find easy access, and the most chearful reception at every house; society without ostentation, good cheer without pride, and every decent diversion which the country affords, with little expense. It is no wonder that the European who has lived here a few years, is desirous to remain; Europe with all its pomp, is not to be compared to this continent, for men of middle stations, or labourers.

An European, when he first arrives, seems limited in his intentions, as well as in his views; but he very suddenly alters his scale; two hundred miles formerly appeared a very great distance, it is now but a trifle; he no sooner breathes our air than he forms schemes, and embarks in designs he never would have thought of in his own country. There the plenitude of society confines many useful ideas, and often extinguishes the most laudable schemes which here ripen into maturity. Thus Europeans become Americans. ...

... It is of very little importance how, and in what manner an indigent man arrives; for if he is but sober, honest, and industrious, he has nothing more to ask of heaven. Let him go to work, he will have opportunities enough to earn a comfortable support, and even the means of procuring some land; which ought to be the utmost wish of every person who has health and hands to work. I knew a man who came to this country, in the literal sense of the expression, stark naked; I think he was a Frenchman, and a sailor on board an

English man-of-war.[1] Being discontented, he had stripped himself and swam ashore; where finding clothes and friends, he settled afterwards at Maraneck, in the county of Chester, in the province of New-York: he married and left a good farm to each of his sons. I knew another person who was but twelve years old when he was taken on the frontiers of Canada by the Indians; at his arrival at Albany he was purchased by a gentleman, who generously bound him apprentice to a tailor. He lived to the age of ninety, and left behind him a fine estate and a numerous family, all well settled; many of them I am acquainted with. Where is then the industrious European who ought to despair?

After a foreigner from any part of Europe is arrived, and become a citizen, let him devoutly listen to the voice of our great parent, which says to him, "Welcome to my shores, distressed European; bless the hour in which thou didst see my verdant fields, my fair navigable rivers, and my green mountains! If thou wilt work, I have bread for thee;[2] if thou wilt be honest, sober, and industrious, I have greater rewards to confer on thee—ease and independence. I will give thee fields to feed and clothe thee; a comfortable fireside to sit by, and tell thy children by what means thou hast prospered; and a decent bed to repose on. I shall endow thee beside with the immunities of a freeman.[3] If thou wilt carefully educate thy children, teach them gratitude to God, and reverence to that government, that philanthropic government, which has collected here so many men and made them happy. I will also provide for thy progeny; and to every good man this ought to be the most holy, the most powerful, the most earnest wish he can possibly form, as well as the most consolatory prospect when he dies. Go thou and work and till; thou shalt prosper, provided thou be just, grateful and industrious." ... In the year 1770, I purchased some lands in the county of ——, which I intended for one of my sons; and was obliged to go there in order to see them properly surveyed and marked out: the soil is good, but the

---

1 *man-of-war* Large warship.
2 *thee* In late eighteenth-century America, the use of *thee* and *thou* as second person singular pronouns was often a sign of membership of the Society of Friends (the Quakers), who had been the first European settlers in Pennsylvania. Farmer James and (especially) his wife use these pronouns with some frequency in certain of the letters.
3 *immunities of a freeman* Rights of a free person.

country has a very wild aspect. However, I observed with pleasure that land sells very fast; and I am in hopes when the lad gets a wife, it will be a well-settled decent country. Agreeable to our customs, which indeed are those of nature, it is our duty to provide for our eldest children while we live, in order that our homesteads may be left to the youngest, who are the most helpless. Some people are apt to regard the portions given to daughters as so much lost to the family; but this is selfish, and is not agreeable to my way of thinking; they cannot work as men do; they marry young: I have given an honest European a farm to till for himself, rent free, provided he clears an acre of swamp every year, and that he quits it whenever my daughter shall marry. It will procure her a substantial husband, a good farmer—and that is all my ambition.

Whilst I was in the woods I met with a party of Indians; I shook hands with them, and I perceived they had killed a cub; I had a little peach brandy, they perceived it also, we therefore joined company, kindled a large fire, and ate an hearty supper. I made their hearts glad, and we all reposed on good beds of leaves. Soon after dark, I was surprised to hear a prodigious hooting through the woods; the Indians laughed heartily. One of them, more skillful than the rest, mimicked the owls so exactly, that a very large one perched on a high tree over our fire. We soon brought him down; he measured five feet seven inches from one extremity of the wings to the other. By Captain —— I have sent you the talons, on which I have had the heads of small candlesticks fixed. Pray keep them on the table of your study for my sake. ...

from Letter 4[1]
Description of the Island of Nantucket, with the Manners, Customs, Policy, and Trade of the Inhabitants

The greatest compliment that can be paid to the best of kings, to the wisest ministers, or the most patriotic rulers, is to think that the reformation of political abuses, and the happiness of their people, are the primary objects of their attention. But alas! how disagreeable must the work of reformation be; how dreaded the operation; for we hear of no amendment; on the contrary, the great number of European emigrants, yearly coming over here, informs us, that the severity of taxes, the injustice of laws, the tyranny of the rich, and the oppressive avarice of the church are as intolerable as ever. Will these calamities have no end? Are not the great rulers of the earth afraid of losing, by degrees, their most useful subjects? This country, providentially intended for the general asylum of the world, will flourish by the oppression of their people; they will every day become better acquainted with the happiness we enjoy, and seek for the means of transporting themselves here, in spite of all obstacles and laws. To what purpose then have so many useful books and divine maxims been transmitted to us from preceding ages? Are they all vain,[2] all useless? Must human nature ever be the sport of the few, and its many wounds remain unhealed? How happy are we here in having fortunately escaped the miseries which attended our fathers; how thankful ought we to be, that they reared us in a land where sobriety and industry never fail to meet with the most ample rewards! You have, no doubt, read several histories of this continent, yet there are a thousand facts, a thousand explanations overlooked. Authors will certainly convey to you a geographical knowledge of this country; they will acquaint you with the eras of the several[3] settlements, the foundations of our towns, the spirit of our different charters, etc., yet they do not sufficiently disclose the genius of the people, their various customs, their modes of agriculture, the innumerable resources which

---

1 *Letter 4* This is the first in a series of five letters dedicated to describing the history, customs, and industry of Nantucket.
2 *vain* Empty; without significance or value.
3 *several* Various and distinctive.

the industrious have of raising themselves to a comfortable and easy situation. Few of these writers have resided here, and those who have had not pervaded every part of the country, nor carefully examined the nature and principles of our association. ... Sensible how unable I am to lead you through so vast a maze, let us look attentively for some small unnoticed corner; but where shall we go in quest of such an one? Numberless settlements, each distinguished by some peculiarities, present themselves on every side; all seem to realise the most sanguine wishes that a good man could form for the happiness of his race. Here they live by fishing on the most plentiful coasts in the world; there they fell trees, by the sides of large rivers, for masts and lumber; here others convert innumerable logs into the best boards; there again others cultivate the land, rear cattle, and clear large fields. Yet I have a spot in my view, where none of these occupations are performed, which will, I hope, reward us for the trouble of inspection; but though it is barren in its soil, insignificant in its extent, inconvenient in its situation, deprived of materials for building; it seems to have been inhabited merely to prove what mankind can do when happily governed! ...

I want not to record the annals of the island of Nantucket—its inhabitants have no annals, for they are not a race of warriors. My simple wish is to trace them throughout their progressive steps, from their arrival here to this present hour; to enquire by what means they have raised themselves from the most humble, the most insignificant beginnings, to the ease and the wealth they now possess; and to give you some idea of their customs, religion, manners, policy, and mode of living.

This happy settlement was not founded on intrusion, forcible entries, or blood, as so many others have been; it drew its origin from necessity on the one side, and from good will on the other; and ever since, all has been a scene of uninterrupted harmony. Neither political, nor religious broils; neither disputes with the natives, nor any other contentions, have in the least agitated or disturbed its detached society. Yet the first founders knew nothing either of Lycurgus or Solon;[1] for this settlement has not been the work of eminent men or powerful legislators, forcing nature by the accumulated labours of art.

---

1 *Lycurgus or Solon* Politicians and reformers of ancient Sparta and Athens, respectively.

This singular establishment has been effected by means of that native industry and perseverance common to all men, when they are protected by a government which demands but little for its protection; when they are permitted to enjoy a system of rational laws founded on perfect freedom. The mildness and humanity of such a government necessarily implies that confidence which is the source of the most arduous undertakings and permanent success. Would you believe that a sandy spot, of about twenty-three thousand acres, affording neither stones nor timber, meadows nor arable, yet can boast of an handsome town, consisting of more than 500 houses, should possess above 200 sail of vessels, constantly employ upwards of 2000 seamen, feed more than 15,000 sheep, 500 cows, 200 horses; and has several citizens worth 20,000 sterling! Yet all these facts are uncontroverted. Who would have imagined that any people should have abandoned a fruitful and extensive continent, filled with the riches which the most ample vegetation affords; replete with good soil, enamelled meadows, rich pastures, every kind of timber, and with all other materials necessary to render life happy and comfortable: to come and inhabit a little sand-bank, to which nature had refused those advantages; to dwell on a spot where there scarcely grew a shrub to announce, by the budding of its leaves, the arrival of the spring, and to warn by their fall the proximity of winter. Had this island been contiguous to the shores of some ancient monarchy, it would only have been occupied by a few wretched fishermen, who, oppressed by poverty, would hardly have been able to purchase or build little fishing barks;[1] always dreading the weight of taxes, or the servitude of men-of-war. Instead of that boldness of speculation for which the inhabitants of this island are so remarkable, they would fearfully have confined themselves, within the narrow limits of the most trifling attempts; timid in their excursions, they never could have extricated themselves from their first difficulties. This island, on the contrary, contains 5000 hardy people, who boldly derive their riches from the element that surrounds them, and have been compelled by the sterility of the soil to seek abroad for the means of subsistence. You must not imagine, from the recital of these facts, that they enjoyed any exclusive privileges or royal charters, or that they were nursed by particular immunities in the infancy of

---

1 *barks* Small boats.

their settlement. No, their freedom, their skill, their probity, and perseverance, have accomplished everything, and brought them by degrees to the rank they now hold. ...

Before I enter into the further detail of this people's government, industry, mode of living, etc., I think it necessary to give you a short sketch of the political state the natives had been in, a few years preceding the arrival of the whites among them. They are hastening towards a total annihilation, and this may be perhaps the last compliment that will ever be paid them by any traveller. They were not extirpated by fraud, violence, or injustice, as hath been the case in so many provinces; on the contrary, they have been treated by these people as brethren; the peculiar genius of their sect inspiring them with the same spirit of moderation which was exhibited at Pennsylvania. Before the arrival of the Europeans, they lived on the fish of their shores; and it was from the same resources the first settlers were compelled to draw their first subsistence. It is uncertain whether the original right of the Earl of Sterling, or that of the Duke of York,[1] was founded on a fair purchase of the soil or not; whatever injustice might have been committed in that respect, cannot be charged to the account of those Friends who purchased from others who no doubt founded their right on Indian grants: and if their numbers are now so decreased, it must not be attributed either to tyranny or violence, but to some of those causes, which have uninterruptedly produced the same effects from one end of the continent to the other, wherever both nations have been mixed. This insignificant spot, like the seashores of the great peninsula, was filled with these people; the great plenty of clams, oysters, and other fish, on which they lived, and which they easily catched, had prodigiously increased their numbers. History does not inform us what particular nation the aborigines of Nantucket were of; it is however very probable that they anciently emigrated from the opposite coast, perhaps from the Hyannees,[2] which is but twenty-seven miles distant. As they then spoke and still

---

1 *Earl of Sterling ... Duke of York* In 1621, James I of England, who was also the Duke of York, granted a vast tract of land (including the island of Nantucket) to William Alexander, 1st Earl of Stirling; Nantucket was deeded to English settler Thomas Mayhew in 1641, seemingly without consultation of the island's Wampanoag inhabitants.
2 *the Hyannees* I.e., Hyannis, on Cape Cod.

speak the Nattick,[1] it is reasonable to suppose that they must have had some affinity with that nation; or else that the Nattick, like the Huron, in the north-western parts of this continent, must have been the most prevailing one in this region. Mr. Elliot,[2] an eminent New England divine, and one of the first founders of that great colony, translated the Bible into this language, in the year 1666, which was printed soon after at Cambridge, near Boston; he translated also the catechism, and many other useful books, which are still very common on this island, and are daily made use of by those Indians who are taught to read. The young Europeans learn it with the same facility as their own tongues; and ever after speak it both with ease and fluency. Whether the present Indians are the descendants of the ancient natives of the island, or whether they are the remains of the many different nations which once inhabited the regions of Mashpè and Nobscusset, in the peninsula now known by the name of Cape Cod; no one can positively tell, not even themselves. The last opinion seems to be that of the most sensible people of the island. So prevailing is the disposition of man to quarrel, and to shed blood; so prone is he to divisions and parties[3] that even the ancient natives of this little spot were separated into two communities, inveterately waging war against each other, like the more powerful tribes of the continent. What do you imagine was the cause of this national quarrel? All the coast of their island equally abounded with the same quantity of fish and clams; in that instance there could be no jealousy, no motives to anger; the country afforded them no game; one would think this ought to have been the country of harmony and peace. But behold the singular destiny of the human kind, ever inferior, in many instances, to the more certain instinct of animals; among which the individuals of the same species are always friends, though reared in different climates: they understand the same language, they shed not each other's blood, they eat not each other's flesh. That part of these rude[4] people who lived on the eastern shores of the island, had from time immemorial tried to destroy those who lived on the west; those

---

1   *Nattick*   Also known as the Massachusett or Wampanoag language.
2   *Mr. Elliot*   Puritan minister John Eliot (1604–90) published a Massachusett translation of the Bible in 1663 as an aid to proselytization.
3   *parties*   Factions.
4   *rude*   Uncivilized.

latter inspired with the same evil genius, had not been behind hand in retaliating: thus was a perpetual war subsisting between these people, founded on no other reason, but the adventitious place of their nativity and residence. In process of time both parties became so thin and depopulated, that the few who remained, fearing lest their race should become totally extinct, fortunately thought of an expedient which prevented their entire annihilation. Some years before the Europeans came, they mutually agreed to settle a partition line which should divide the island from north to south; the people of the west agreed not to kill those of the east, except they were found transgressing over the western part of the line; those of the last entered into a reciprocal agreement. By these simple means peace was established among them, and this is the only record which seems to entitle them to the denomination of men. This happy settlement put a stop to their sanguinary depredations, none fell afterward but a few rash imprudent individuals; on the contrary, they multiplied greatly. But another misfortune awaited them; when the Europeans came they caught the small pox, and their improper treatment of that disorder swept away great numbers: this calamity was succeeded by the use of rum; and these are the two principal causes which so much diminished their numbers, not only here but all over the continent. In some places whole nations have disappeared. Some years ago three Indian canoes, on their return to Detroit from the falls of Niagara, unluckily got the smallpox from the Europeans with whom they had traded. It broke out near the long point on Lake Erie, there they all perished; their canoes, and their goods, were afterwards found by some travellers journeying the same way; their dogs were still alive. Besides the smallpox, and the use of spirituous liquors, the two greatest curses they have received from us, there is a sort of physical antipathy, which is equally powerful from one end of the continent to the other. Wherever they happen to be mixed, or even to live in the neighbourhood of the Europeans, they become exposed to a variety of accidents and misfortunes to which they always fall victims: such are particular fevers, to which they were strangers before, and sinking into a singular sort of indolence and sloth. This has been invariably the case wherever the same association has taken place; as at Nattick, Mashpè, Soccanoket in the bounds of Falmouth, Nobscusset, Houratonick,

Monhauset, and the Vineyard.[1] Even the Mohawks themselves, who were once so populous, and such renowned warriors, are now reduced to less than 200 since the European settlements have circumscribed the territories which their ancestors had reserved. Three years before the arrival of the Europeans at Cape Cod, a frightful distemper had swept away a great many along its coasts, which made the landing and intrusion of our forefathers much easier than it otherwise might have been. In the year 1763, above half of the Indians of this island perished by a strange fever, which the Europeans who nursed them never caught; they appear to be a race doomed to recede and disappear before the superior genius of the Europeans. The only ancient custom of these people that is remembered is, that in their mutual exchanges forty sun-dried clams, strung on a string, passed for the value of what might be called a copper.[2] They were strangers to the use and value of wampum, so well known to those of the main. The few families now remaining are meek and harmless; their ancient ferocity is gone: they were early christianized by the New England missionaries, as well as those of the Vineyard, and of several other parts of Massachusetts; and to this day they remain strict observers of the laws and customs of that religion, being carefully taught while young. Their sedentary life has led them to this degree of civilization much more effectually than if they had still remained hunters. They are fond of the sea, and expert mariners. They have learned from the Quakers the art of catching both the cod and whale, in consequence of which five of them always make part of the complement of men requisite to fit out a whale-boat. Many have removed hither from the Vineyard, on which account they are more numerous on Nantucket, than anywhere else.

It is strange what revolution has happened among them in less than two hundred years! What is become of those numerous tribes which formerly inhabited the extensive shores of the great bay of Massachusetts? Even from Numkeag (*Salem*), Saugus (*Lynn*), Shawmut (*Boston*), Pataxet, Napouset (*Milton*), Matapan (*Dorchester*), Winèsimèt (*Chelsea*), Poïasset, Pokànoket (*New Plymouth*), Suecanosset (*Falmouth*), Titicut (*Chatham*), Nobscusset (*Yarmouth*), Naussit (*Eartham*), Hyanneès (*Barnstable*), etc., and many others

---

1   *the Vineyard*   I.e., Martha's Vineyard.
2   *copper*   Penny; one-cent coin.

who lived on sea-shores of above three hundred miles in length; without mentioning those powerful tribes which once dwelt between the rivers Hudson, Connecticut, Piskàtàquà, and Kènnebèck, the Mèhikaudret, Mohiguine, Pèquods, Narragansets, Nianticks, Massachusetts, Wamponougs, Nipnets, Tarranteens, etc. They are gone, and every memorial of them is lost; no vestiges whatever are left of those swarms which once inhabited this country, and replenished both sides of the great peninsula of Cape Cod: not even one of the posterity of the famous Masconomèo[1] is left (the sachem of Cape Ann); not one of the descendants of Massasoit, father of Mètacomèt (*Philip*), and Wamsutta (*Alexander*), he who first conveyed some lands to the Plymouth Company.[2] They have all disappeared either in the wars which the Europeans carried on against them, or else they have mouldered away, gathered in some of their ancient towns, in contempt and oblivion: nothing remains of them all, but one extraordinary monument, and even this they owe to the industry and religious zeal of the Europeans, I mean the Bible translated into the Nattick tongue. Many of these tribes, giving way to the superior power of the whites, retired to their ancient villages, collecting the scattered remains of nations once populous; and in their grant of lands reserved to themselves and posterity certain portions, which lay contiguous to them. There forgetting their ancient manners, they dwelt in peace; in a few years their territories were surrounded by the improvements of the Europeans; in consequence of which they grew lazy, inactive, unwilling, and unapt to imitate, or to follow any of our trades, and in a few generations either totally perished or else came over to the Vineyard, or to this island, to re-unite themselves with such societies of their countrymen as would receive them. Such has been the fate of many nations, once warlike and independent; what we see now on the main, or on those islands, may be justly considered as the only remains of those ancient tribes. Might I be permitted to pay perhaps

---

1   *Masconomèo*   Better known in English as Masconomet, sachem or chief of the Agawam people, who ceded a vast tract of territorial land to English settlers in the 1630s.

2   *Massasoit ... Plymouth Company*   Crèvecoeur refers to a family of influential Wampanoag sachems who dealt extensively with New England settlers throughout the seventeenth century. Wamsutta, known by the English as Alexander, became sachem in 1661 following his father Massasoit's death; Wamsutta's own death in 1662 saw Wampanoag leadership passed on to Metacom, widely known by the English as King Philip and a central figure in the war of resistance known as King Philip's War (1775–78).

a very useless compliment to *those* at least who inhabited the great peninsula of Namset, now Cape Cod, with whose names and ancient situation I am well acquainted. This peninsula was divided into two great regions; that on the side of the bay was known by the name of Nobscusset, from one of its towns; the capital was called Nausit (*now Eastham*); hence the Indians of that region were called Nausit Indians, though they dwelt in the villages of Pamet, Nosset, Pashèe, Potomaket, Soktoowoket, Nobscusset (*Yarmouth*).

The region on the Atlantic side was called Mashpèe, and contained the tribes of Hyannèes, Costowet, Waquoit, Scootin, Saconasset, Mashpèe, and Namset. Several of these Indian towns have been since converted into flourishing European settlements, known by different names; for as the natives were excellent judges of land, which they had fertilized besides with the shells of their fish, etc., the latter could not make a better choice; though in general this great peninsula is but a sandy pine track, a few good spots excepted. It is divided into seven townships, viz. Barnstable, Yarmouth, Harwich, Chatham, Eastham, Pamet, Namset, or Province town, at the extremity of the Cape. Yet these are very populous, though I am at a loss to conceive on what the inhabitants live, besides clams, oysters, and fish; their piny lands being the most ungrateful soil in the world. The minister of Namset or Province Town, receives from the government of Massachusetts a salary of fifty pounds per annum; and such is the poverty of the inhabitants of that place, that, unable to pay him any money, each master of a family is obliged to allow him two hundred horse feet (*sea spin*)[1] with which this primitive priest fertilizes the land of his glebe,[2] which he tills himself: for nothing will grow on these hungry soils without the assistance of this extraordinary manure, fourteen bushels of Indian corn being looked upon as a good crop. But it is time to return from a digression, which I hope you will pardon. Nantucket is a great nursery of seamen, pilots, coasters, and bank-fishermen; as a country belonging to the province of Massachusetts, it has yearly the benefit of a court of Common Pleas, and their appeal lies to the

---

1 *horse feet (sea spin)* Plant now more commonly known as *coltsfoot*, the flowers of which are still used as fertilizer in some parts of northeastern North America. ("Sea spin" was presumably an alternative name for the same plant.)

2 *glebe* Field; patch of earth.

supreme court at Boston. I observed before, that the Friends[1] compose two thirds of the magistracy of this island; thus they are the proprietors of its territory, and the principal rulers of its inhabitants; but with all this apparatus of law, its coercive powers are seldom wanted or required. Seldom is it that any individual is amerced[2] or punished; their jail conveys no terror; no man has lost his life here judicially since the foundation of this town, which is upwards of an hundred years. Solemn tribunals, public executions, humiliating punishments, are altogether unknown. I saw neither governors nor any pageantry of state; neither ostentatious magistrates nor any individuals clothed with useless dignity: no artificial phantoms subsist here, either civil or religious; no gibbets[3] loaded with guilty citizens offer themselves to your view; no soldiers are appointed to bayonet their compatriots into servile compliance. But how is a society composed of 5,000 individuals preserved in the bonds of peace and tranquility? How are the weak protected from the strong? I will tell you. Idleness and poverty, the causes of so many crimes, are unknown here; each seeks in the prosecution of his lawful business that honest gain which supports them; every period of their time is full, either on shore or at sea. A probable expectation of reasonable profits, or of kindly assistance, if they fail of success, renders them strangers to licentious expedients. The simplicity of their manners shortens the catalogue of their wants; the law at a distance is ever ready to exert itself in the protection of those who stand in need of its assistance. The greatest part of them are always at sea, pursuing the whale or raising the cod from the surface of the banks: some cultivate their little farms with the utmost diligence; some are employed in exercising various trades; others again in providing every necessary resource in order to refit their vessels, or repair what misfortunes may happen, looking out for future markets, etc. Such is the rotation of those different scenes of business which fill the measure of their days; of that part of their lives at least which is enlivened by health, spirits, and vigour. It is but seldom that vice grows on a barren sand like this, which produces nothing without extreme labour. How could the common follies of society take root in so despicable a soil; they generally thrive on its exuberant juices:

---

1   *Friends*   I.e., Quakers, formally known as the Society of Friends.
2   *amerced*   Fined.
3   *gibbets*   Instruments for publicly displaying the bodies of executed criminals.

here there are none but those which administer to the useful, to the necessary, and to the indispensable comforts of life. This land must necessarily either produce health, temperance, and a great equality of conditions, or the most abject misery. Could the manners of luxurious countries be imported here, like an epidemical disorder they would destroy everything; the majority of them could not exist a month, they would be obliged to emigrate. As in all societies except that of the natives, some difference must necessarily exist between individual and individual, for there must be some more exalted than the rest either by their riches or their talents; so in *this*, there are what you might call the high, the middling, and the low; and this difference will always be more remarkable among people who live by sea excursions than among those who live by the cultivation of their land. The first run greater hazard, and adventure more: the profits and the misfortunes attending this mode of life must necessarily introduce a greater disparity than among the latter, where the equal divisions of the land offers no short road to superior riches. The only difference that may arise among them is that of industry, and perhaps of superior goodness of soil: the gradations I observed here, are founded on nothing more than the good or ill success of their maritime enterprizes, and do not proceed from education; that is the same throughout every class, simple, useful, and unadorned like their dress and their houses. This necessary difference in their fortunes does not however cause those heart burnings, which in other societies generate crimes. The sea which surrounds them is equally open to all, and presents to all an equal title to the chance of good fortune. A collector from Boston is the only king's officer who appears on these shores to receive the trifling duties which this community owe to those who protect them, and under the shadow of whose wings they navigate to all parts of the world.

DESCRIPTION OF CHARLES-TOWN;[1] THOUGHTS ON SLAVERY; ON PHYSICAL EVIL; A MELANCHOLY SCENE

Charles-Town is, in the north, what Lima is in the south; both are capitals of the richest provinces of their respective hemispheres: you may therefore conjecture that both cities must exhibit the appearances necessarily resulting from riches. Peru abounding in gold, Lima is filled with inhabitants who enjoy all those gradations of pleasure, refinement, and luxury, which proceed from wealth. Carolina produces commodities more valuable perhaps than gold, because they are gained by greater industry; it exhibits also on our northern stage a display of riches and luxury, inferior indeed to the former, but far superior to what are to be seen in our northern towns. Its situation is admirable, being built at the confluence of two large rivers, which receive in their course a great number of inferior streams; all navigable in the spring, for flat boats. Here the produce of this extensive territory concentres; here therefore is the seat of the most valuable exportation; their wharfs, their docks, their magazines,[2] are extremely convenient to facilitate this great commercial business. The inhabitants are the gayest in America; it is called the centre of our beau monde, and is always filled with the richest planters of the province, who resort hither in quest of health and pleasure. Here are always to be seen a great number of valetudinarians from the West Indies, seeking for the renovation of health, exhausted by the debilitating nature of their sun, air, and modes of living. Many of these West Indians have I seen, at thirty, loaded with the infirmities of old age; for nothing is more common in those countries of wealth, than for persons to lose the abilities of enjoying the comforts of life, at a time when we northern men just begin to taste the fruits of our labour and prudence. The round of pleasure, and the expenses of those citizens' tables, are much superior to what you would imagine: indeed the growth of this town and province have been astonishingly rapid. It is pity that the narrowness of the neck on which it stands prevents it from increasing; and which is the reason why houses are so dear.

---

1 *DESCRIPTION OF CHARLES-TOWN* It is likely that Crèvecoeur himself never traveled to South Carolina, and that what knowledge he had of the region was second-hand.

2 *magazines* Storehouses.

The heat of the climate, which is sometimes very great in the interior parts of the country, is always temperate in Charles-Town; though sometimes when they have no sea breezes the sun is too powerful. The climate renders excesses of all kinds very dangerous, particularly those of the table; and yet, insensible or fearless of danger, they live on, and enjoy a short and a merry life: the rays of their sun seem to urge them irresistibly to dissipation and pleasure: on the contrary, the women, from being abstemious,[1] reach to a longer period of life, and seldom die without having had several husbands. An European at his first arrival must be greatly surprised when he sees the elegance of their houses, their sumptuous furniture, as well as the magnificence of their tables; can he imagine himself in a country, the establishment of which is so recent?

The three principal classes of inhabitants are lawyers, planters, and merchants; this is the province which has afforded to the first the richest spoils, for nothing can exceed their wealth, their power, and their influence. They have reached the *ne plus ultra*[2] of worldly felicity; no plantation is secured, no title is good, no will is valid, but what they dictate, regulate, and approve. The whole mass of provincial property is become tributary to this society—which, far above priests and bishops, disdain to be satisfied with the poor Mosaical portion of the tenth.[3] I appeal to the many inhabitants, who, while contending perhaps for their right to a few hundred acres, have lost by the mazes of the law their whole patrimony. These men are more properly law givers than interpreters of the law; and have united here, as well as in most other provinces, the skill and dexterity of the scribe with the power and ambition of the prince: who can tell where this may lead in a future day? The nature of our laws, and the spirit of freedom, which often tends to make us litigious,[4] must necessarily throw the greatest part of the property of the colonies into the hands of these gentlemen. In another century, the law will possess in the north, what now the church possesses in Peru and Mexico.

---

1   *abstemious*   Moderate in their habits.
2   *ne plus ultra*   Highest point; pinnacle.
3   *the poor … tenth*   I.e., tithes, taxes paid to the church equivalent to one-tenth of one's annual earnings. Tithe laws are set out in the Old Testament or the Torah as part of what is called Mosaic Law.
4   *litigious*   Inclined towards having disputes, particularly legal disputes.

While all is joy, festivity, and happiness in Charles-Town, would you imagine that scenes of misery overspread in the country? Their ears by habit are become deaf, their hearts are hardened; they neither see, hear, nor feel for the woes of their poor slaves, from whose painful labours all their wealth proceeds. Here the horrors of slavery, the hardship of incessant toils, are unseen; and no one thinks with compassion of those showers of sweat and of tears which from the bodies of Africans daily drop, and moisten the ground they till. The cracks of the whip urging these miserable beings to excessive labour, are far too distant from the gay Capital to be heard. The chosen race eat, drink, and live happy, while the unfortunate one grubs up the ground, raises indigo, or husks the rice; exposed to a sun full as scorching as their native one; without the support of good food, without the cordials of any cheering liquor. This great contrast has often afforded me subjects of the most afflicting meditation. On the one side, behold a people enjoying all that life affords most bewitching and pleasurable, without labour, without fatigue, hardly subjected to the trouble of wishing. With gold, dug from Peruvian mountains, they order vessels to the coasts of Guinea; by virtue of that gold, wars, murders, and devastations are committed in some harmless, peaceable African neighbourhood, where dwelt innocent people, who even knew not but that all men were black.[1] The daughter torn from her weeping mother, the child from the wretched parents, the wife from the loving husband; whole families swept away and brought through storms and tempests to this rich metropolis! There, arranged like horses at a fair, they are branded like cattle, and then driven to toil, to starve, and to languish for a few years on the different plantations of these citizens. And for whom must they work? For persons they know not, and who have no other power over them than that of violence; no other right than what this accursed metal has given them! Strange order of things! Oh, Nature, where art thou? Are not these blacks thy children as well as we? On the other side, nothing is to be seen but the most diffusive misery and wretchedness, unrelieved even in thought or wish! Day after day they drudge on without any prospect of ever reaping for themselves; they are obliged to devote their lives, their limbs, their will, and every vital exertion to swell the wealth of masters; who look

---

1   *who even ... black* I.e., who did not even know that not all men are black.

not upon them with half the kindness and affection with which they consider their dogs and horses. Kindness and affection are not the portion of those who till the earth, who carry burdens, who convert the logs into useful boards. This reward, simple and natural as one would conceive it, would border on humanity; and planters must have none of it!

If negroes are permitted to become fathers, this fatal indulgence only tends to increase their misery: the poor companions of their scanty pleasures are likewise the companions of their labours; and when at some critical seasons they could wish to see them relieved, with tears in their eyes they behold them perhaps doubly oppressed, obliged to bear the burden of nature—a fatal present—as well as that of unabated tasks. How many have I seen cursing the irresistible propensity, and regretting that, by having tasted of those harmless joys, they had become the authors of double misery to their wives. Like their masters, they are not permitted to partake of those ineffable sensations with which nature inspires the hearts of fathers and mothers; they must repel them all, and become callous and passive. This unnatural state often occasions the most acute, the most pungent of their afflictions; they have no time, like us, tenderly to rear their helpless offspring, to nurse them on their knees, to enjoy the delight of being parents. Their paternal fondness is embittered by considering that, if their children live, they must live to be slaves like themselves; no time is allowed them to exercise their pious office.[1] The mothers must fasten them on their backs, and, with this double load, follow their husbands in the fields, where they too often hear no other sound than that of the voice or whip of the task-master, and the cries of their infants, broiling in the sun. These unfortunate creatures cry and weep like their parents, without a possibility of relief; the very instinct of the brute, so laudable, so irresistible, runs counter here to their master's interest; and to that god all the laws of nature must give way. Thus planters get rich; so raw, so unexperienced am I in this mode of life, that were I to be possessed of a plantation, and my slaves treated as in general they are here, never could I rest in peace; my sleep would be perpetually disturbed by a retrospect of the frauds committed in Africa, in order to entrap them; frauds surpassing in enormity

---

1   *office*   Role; duty.

everything which a common mind can possibly conceive. I should be thinking of the barbarous treatment they meet with on shipboard; of their anguish, of the despair necessarily inspired by their situation, when torn from their friends and relations; when delivered into the hands of a people differently coloured, whom they cannot understand; carried in a strange machine over an ever agitated element, which they had never seen before; and finally delivered over to the severities of the whippers, and the excessive labours of the field. Can it be possible that the force of custom should ever make me deaf to all these reflections, and as insensible to the injustice of that trade, and to their miseries, as the rich inhabitants of this town seem to be? What then is man; this being who boasts so much of the excellence and dignity of his nature, among that variety of inscrutable mysteries, of unsolvable problems with which he is surrounded? The reason why man has been thus created is not the least astonishing! It is said, I know, that they are much happier here than in the West-Indies; because land being cheaper upon this continent than in those islands, the fields allowed them to raise their subsistence from are in general more extensive. The only possible chance of any alleviation depends on the humour of the planters, who, bred in the midst of slaves, learn from the example of their parents to despise them; and seldom conceive either from religion or philosophy any ideas that tend to make their fate less calamitous; except[1] some strong native tenderness of heart, some rays of philanthropy, overcome the obduracy[2] contracted by habit.

I have not resided here long enough to become insensible of pain for the objects which I every day behold. In the choice of my friends and acquaintance, I always endeavour to find out those whose dispositions are somewhat congenial with my own. We have slaves likewise in our northern provinces;[3] I hope the time draws near when they will be all emancipated: but how different their lot, how different their situation, in every possible respect! They enjoy as much liberty as their masters, they are as well clad, and as well fed; in health and

---

1 *except* Unless.
2 *obduracy* Inability to be moved by pity; hard-heartedness.
3 *We have ... northern provinces* Pennsylvania (the home state of Farmer James) began a process of gradual abolition in 1780; New York State (Crèvecoeur's residence while he was writing the bulk of the *Letters*) did likewise in 1799. The last enslaved people in New York State were not freed until 1827.

sickness they are tenderly taken care of; they live under the same roof, and are, truly speaking, a part of our families. Many of them are taught to read and write, and are well instructed in the principles of religion; they are the companions of our labours, and treated as such; they enjoy many perquisites,[1] many established holidays, and are not obliged to work more than white people. They marry where inclination leads them; visit their wives every week; are as decently clad as the common people; they are indulged in educating, cherishing, and chastising their children, who are taught subordination to them as to their lawful parents. In short, they participate in many of the benefits of our society, without being obliged to bear any of its burdens. They are fat, healthy, and hearty, and far from repining at their fate; they think themselves happier than many of the lower class whites: they share with their masters the wheat and meat provision they help to raise; many of those whom the good Quakers have emancipated have received that great benefit with tears of regret, and have never quitted, though free, their former masters and benefactors.

But is it really true, as I have heard it asserted here, that those blacks are incapable of feeling the spurs of emulation,[2] and the cheerful sound of encouragement? By no means; there are a thousand proofs existing of their gratitude and fidelity: those hearts in which such noble dispositions can grow, are then like ours, they are susceptible of every generous sentiment, of every useful motive of action; they are capable of receiving lights, of imbibing ideas that would greatly alleviate the weight of their miseries. But what methods have in general been made use of to obtain so desirable an end? None; the day in which they arrive and are sold, is the first of their labours; labours, which from that hour admit of no respite; for though indulged by law with relaxation on Sundays, they are obliged to employ that time which is intended for rest, to till their little plantations.[3] What can be expected from wretches in such circumstances?

---

1   *enjoy many perquisites*   I.e., receive many rewards or forms of compensation for their labor.
2   *emulation*   Ambition.
3   *indulged by law ... plantations*   In many areas, enslaved people were legally required to be given "leisure time" from their ordinary labor on Sundays, a fact held up by many enslavers as proof that American slavery was not as cruel as their opponents claimed; however, as the narrator here points out, enslaved individuals generally had to use this time for the tending of their own small vegetable allotments and for other tasks required for their sustenance.

Forced from their native country, cruelly treated when on board, and not less so on the plantations to which they are driven; is there anything in this treatment but what must kindle all the passions, sow the seeds of inveterate resentment, and nourish a wish of perpetual revenge? They are left to the irresistible effects of those strong and natural propensities; the blows they receive, are they conducive to extinguish them, or to win their affections? They are neither soothed by the hopes that their slavery will ever terminate but with their lives; [n]or yet encouraged by the goodness of their food, or the mildness of their treatment. The very hopes held out to mankind by religion, that consolatory system so useful to the miserable, are never presented to them; neither moral nor physical means are made use of to soften their chains; they are left in their original and untutored state, that very state wherein the natural propensities of revenge and warm passions are so soon kindled. Cheered by no one single motive that can impel the will, or excite their efforts, nothing but terrors and punishments are presented to them; death is denounced[1] if they run away; horrid dilaceration[2] if they speak with their native freedom; perpetually awed by the terrible cracks of whips, or by the fear of capital punishments, while even those punishments often fail of their purpose.

A clergyman settled a few years ago at George-Town, and feeling as I do now, warmly recommended to the planters, from the pulpit, a relaxation of severity; he introduced the benignity of Christianity, and pathetically made use of the admirable precepts of that system to melt the hearts of his congregation into a greater degree of compassion toward their slaves than had been hitherto customary; "Sir (said one of his hearers) we pay you a genteel salary to read to us the prayers of the liturgy, and to explain to us such parts of the Gospel as the rule of the church directs; but we do not want you to teach us what we are to do with our blacks." The clergyman found it prudent to withhold any farther admonition. Whence this astonishing right, or rather this barbarous custom, for most certainly we have no kind of right beyond that of force? We are told, it is true, that slavery cannot be so repugnant to human nature as we at first imagine, because it

---

1   *denounced*   Threatened.
2   *dilaceration*   Tearing of the body; i.e., severe physical abuse.

has been practised in all ages, and in all nations: the Lacedemonians themselves, those great assertors of liberty, conquered the Helotes with the design of making them their slaves;[1] the Romans, whom we consider as our masters in civil and military policy, lived in the exercise of the most horrid oppression; they conquered to plunder and to enslave. What a hideous aspect the face of the earth must then have exhibited! Provinces, towns, districts, often depopulated; their inhabitants driven to Rome, the greatest market in the world, and there sold by thousands! The Roman dominions were tilled by the hands of unfortunate people, who had once been, like their victors free, rich, and possessed of every benefit society can confer; until they became subject to the cruel right of war, and to lawless force. Is there then no superintending power who conducts the moral operations of the world, as well as the physical? The same sublime hand which guides the planets round the sun with so much exactness, which preserves the arrangement of the whole with such exalted wisdom and paternal care, and prevents the vast system from falling into confusion; doth it abandon mankind to all the errors, the follies, and the miseries, which their most frantic rage, and their most dangerous vices and passions can produce?

The history of the earth! doth it present anything but crimes of the most heinous nature, committed from one end of the world to the other? We observe avarice, rapine,[2] and murder, equally prevailing in all parts. History perpetually tells us of millions of people abandoned to the caprice of the maddest princes, and of whole nations devoted to the blind fury of tyrants. Countries destroyed; nations alternately buried in ruins by other nations; some parts of the world beautifully cultivated, returned again to the pristine state; the fruits of ages of industry, the toil of thousands in a short time destroyed by few! If one corner breathes in peace for a few years, it is, in turn subjected, torn, and levelled; one would almost believe the principles of action in man, considered as the first agent of this planet, to be poisoned in their most essential parts. We certainly are not that class of beings

---

1 *Lacedemonians ... their slaves* The Helots were a class of people subjugated by the Lacedemonians (or the Spartans) in the ancient world. Historians have long debated whether the Helots were truly members of an enslaved class or whether their status was something between that of enslaved and free.
2 *rapine* Plunder.

which we vainly think ourselves to be; man an animal of prey, seems to have rapine and the love of bloodshed implanted in his heart; nay, to hold it the most honourable occupation in society: we never speak of a hero of mathematics, a hero of knowledge or humanity; no, this illustrious appellation is reserved for the most successful butchers of the world. If Nature has given us a fruitful soil to inhabit, she has refused us such inclinations and propensities as would afford us the full enjoyment of it. Extensive as the surface of this planet is, not one half of it is yet cultivated, not half replenished; she created man, and placed him either in the woods or plains, and provided him with passions which must forever oppose his happiness: everything is submitted to the power of the strongest; men, like the elements, are always at war; the weakest yield to the most potent; force, subtilty, and malice, always triumph over unguarded honesty, and simplicity. Benignity, moderation, and justice, are virtues adapted only to the humble paths of life: we love to talk of virtue and to admire its beauty, while in the shade of solitude, and retirement; but when we step forth into active life, if it happen to be in competition with any passion or desire, do we observe it to prevail? Hence so many religious impostors have triumphed over the credulity of mankind, and have rendered their frauds the creeds of succeeding generations, during the course of many ages; until worn away by time, they have been replaced by new ones. Hence the most unjust war, if supported by the greatest force, always succeeds; hence the most just ones, when supported only by their justice, as often fail. Such is the ascendancy of power; the supreme arbiter of all the revolutions which we observe in this planet: so irresistible is power, that it often thwarts the tendency of the most forcible causes, and prevents their subsequent salutary effects, though ordained for the good of man by the Governor of the universe. Such is the perverseness of human nature; who can describe it in all its latitude?

In the moments of our philanthropy we often talk of an indulgent nature, a kind parent, who for the benefit of mankind has taken singular pains to vary the genera of plants, fruits, grain, and the different productions of the earth, and has spread peculiar blessings in each climate. This is undoubtedly an object of contemplation which calls forth our warmest gratitude; for so singularly benevolent have those parental intentions been, that where barrenness of soil or severity of

climate prevail, there she has implanted in the heart of man sentiments which overbalance every misery, and supply the place of every
want. She has given to the inhabitants of these regions an attachment to their savage rocks and wild shores, unknown to those who
inhabit the fertile fields of the temperate zone. Yet if we attentively
view this globe, will it not appear rather a place of punishment than
of delight? And what misfortune! that those punishments should fall
on the innocent, and its few delights be enjoyed by the most unworthy. Famine, diseases, elementary convulsions, human feuds, dissen-
sions, etc., are the produce of every climate; each climate produces,
besides, vices and miseries peculiar to its latitude. View the frigid
sterility of the north, whose famished inhabitants, hardly acquainted
with the sun, live and fare worse than the bears they hunt—and to
which they are superior only in the faculty of speaking. View the
arctic and antarctic regions, those huge voids where nothing lives;
regions of eternal snow; where winter in all his horrors has established
his throne, and arrested every creative power of nature. Will you call
the miserable stragglers in these countries by the name of men? Now
contrast this frigid power of the north and south with that of the sun;
examine the parched lands of the torrid zone, replete with sulphure-
ous exhalations; view those countries of Asia subject to pestilential
infections which lay nature waste; view this globe often convulsed
both from within and without; pouring forth from several mouths,
rivers of boiling matter, which are imperceptibly leaving immense
subterranean graves, wherein millions will one day perish! Look at the
poisonous soil of the equator, at those putrid slimy tracks, teeming
with horrid monsters, the enemies of the human race; look next at
the sandy continent, scorched perhaps by the fatal approach of some
ancient comet, now the abode of desolation. Examine the rains, the
convulsive storms of those climates, where masses of sulphur, bitu-
men, and electrical fire, combining their dreadful powers, are incessantly hovering and bursting over a globe threatened with dissolution.
On this little shell, how very few are the spots where man can live
and flourish! Even under those mild climates which seem to breathe
peace and happiness, the poison of slavery, the fury of despotism, and
the rage of superstition, are all combined against man! There only
the few live and rule, whilst the many starve and utter ineffectual
complaints: there, human nature appears more debased perhaps than

in the less favoured climates. The fertile plains of Asia, the rich low lands of Egypt and of Diarbeck,[1] the fruitful fields bordering on the Tigris and the Euphrates,[2] the extensive country of the East Indies in all its separate districts; all these must to the geographical eye seem as if intended for terrestrial paradises: but though surrounded with the spontaneous riches of nature, though her kindest favours seem to be shed on those beautiful regions with the most profuse hand, yet there in general we find the most wretched people in the world. Almost everywhere, liberty, so natural to mankind, is refused, or rather enjoyed but by their tyrants; the word slave is the appellation of every rank, who adore as a divinity a being worse than themselves; subject to every caprice, and to every lawless rage which unrestrained power can give. Tears are shed, perpetual groans are heard, where only the accents of peace, alacrity, and gratitude should resound. There the very delirium of tyranny tramples on the best gifts of nature, and sports with the fate, the happiness, the lives of millions: there the extreme fertility of the ground always indicates the extreme misery of the inhabitants!

Everywhere one part of the human species are taught the art of shedding the blood of the other; of setting fire to their dwellings; of levelling the works of their industry: half of the existence of nations regularly employed in destroying other nations. What little political felicity is to be met with here and there has cost oceans of blood to purchase; as if good was never to be the portion of unhappy man. Republics, kingdoms, monarchies, founded either on fraud or successful violence, increase by pursuing the steps of the same policy, until they are destroyed in their turn, either by the influence of their own crimes, or by more successful but equally criminal enemies.

If from this general review of human nature, we descend to the examination of what is called civilized society; there the combination of every natural and artificial want, makes us pay very dear for what little share of political felicity we enjoy. It is a strange heterogeneous assemblage of vices and virtues, and of a variety of other principles, forever at war, forever jarring, forever producing some dangerous, some distressing extreme. Where do you conceive then that nature

---

1 *Diarbeck* Diyarbakir, significant city in Turkey.
2 *Tigris and the Euphrates* River system in western Asia; part of a historically significant region known as the Fertile Crescent.

intended we should be happy? Would you prefer the state of men in the woods, to that of men in a more improved situation? Evil preponderates in both; in the first they often eat each other for want of food, and in the other they often starve each other for want of room. For my part, I think the vices and miseries to be found in the latter, exceed those of the former; in which real evil is more scarce, more supportable, and less enormous. Yet we wish to see the earth peopled; to accomplish the happiness of kingdoms, which is said to consist in numbers. Gracious God! to what end is the introduction of so many beings into a mode of existence in which they must grope amidst as many errors, commit as many crimes, and meet with as many diseases, wants, and sufferings!

The following scene will I hope account for these melancholy reflections, and apologize for the gloomy thoughts with which I have filled this letter: my mind is, and always has been, oppressed since I became a witness to it. I was not long since invited to dine with a planter who lived three miles from ——, where he then resided. In order to avoid the heat of the sun, I resolved to go on foot, sheltered in a small path, leading through a pleasant wood. I was leisurely travelling along, attentively examining some peculiar plants which I had collected, when all at once I felt the air strongly agitated; though the day was perfectly calm and sultry. I immediately cast my eyes toward the cleared ground, from which I was but at a small distance, in order to see whether it was not occasioned by a sudden shower; when at that instant a sound resembling a deep rough voice, uttered, as I thought, a few inarticulate monosyllables. Alarmed and surprized, I precipitately looked all round, when I perceived at about six rods distance[1] something resembling a cage, suspended to the limbs of a tree; all the branches of which appeared covered with large birds of prey, fluttering about, and anxiously endeavouring to perch on the cage. Actuated by an involuntary motion of my hands more than by any design of my mind, I fired at them; they all flew to a short distance, with a most hideous noise: when, horrid to think and painful to repeat, I perceived a negro, suspended in the cage, and left there to expire! I shudder when I recollect that the birds had already picked out his eyes; his cheek bones were bare; his arms had been attacked

---

1   *at about ... rods distance*   About thirty yards away.

in several places, and his body seemed covered with a multitude of wounds. From the edges of the hollow sockets and from the lacerations with which he was disfigured, the blood slowly dropped, and tinged the ground beneath. No sooner were the birds flown, than swarms of insects covered the whole body of this unfortunate wretch, eager to feed on his mangled flesh and to drink his blood. I found myself suddenly arrested by the power of affright and terror; my nerves were convulsed; I trembled, I stood motionless, involuntarily contemplating the fate of this negro, in all its dismal latitude. The living spectre, though deprived of his eyes, could still distinctly hear, and in his uncouth dialect begged me to give him some water to allay his thirst. Humanity herself would have recoiled back with horror; she would have balanced whether to lessen such reliefless distress, or mercifully with one blow to end this dreadful scene of agonizing torture! Had I had a ball in my gun, I certainly should have dispatched[1] him; but finding myself unable to perform so kind an office, I sought, though trembling, to relieve him as well as I could. A shell ready fixed to a pole, which had been used by some negroes, presented itself to me; filled it with water, and with trembling hands I guided it to the quivering lips of the wretched sufferer. Urged by the irresistible power of thirst, he endeavoured to meet it, as he instinctively guessed its approach by the noise it made in passing through the bars of the cage. "Tankè, you whitè man, tankè you, puté somè poyson and givè me." How long have you been hanging there? I asked him. "Two days, and me no die; the birds, the birds; aaah me!" Oppressed with the reflections which this shocking spectacle afforded me, I mustered strength enough to walk away, and soon reached the house at which I intended to dine. There I heard that the reason for this slave being thus punished, was on account of his having killed the overseer of the plantation. They told me that the laws of self-preservation rendered such executions necessary; and supported the doctrine of slavery with the arguments generally made use of to justify the practice; with the repetition of which I shall not trouble you at present.

Adieu.

---

1   *dispatched*   Killed.

from LETTER 10
ON SNAKES; AND ON THE HUMMINGBIRD

Why would you prescribe this talk; you know that what we take up ourselves seems always lighter than what is imposed on us by others. You insist on my saying something about our snakes; and in relating what I know concerning them, were it not for two singularities, the one of which I saw, and the other I received from an eye-witness, I should have but very little to observe. The southern provinces are the countries where nature has formed the greatest variety of alligators, snakes, serpents; and scorpions, from the smallest size, up to the *pine barren*, the largest species known here. We have but two, whose stings are mortal, which deserve to be mentioned; as for the black one, it is remarkable for nothing but its industry, agility, beauty, and the art of enticing birds by the power of its eyes. I admire it much, and never kill it, though its formidable length and appearance often get the better of the philosophy of some people, particularly of Europeans. The most dangerous one is the *pilot*, or *copperhead*; for the poison of which no remedy has yet been discovered. It bears the first name because it always precedes the rattlesnake; that is, quits its state of torpidity in the spring a week before the other. It bears the second name on account of its head being adorned with many copper-coloured spots. It lurks in rocks near the water, and is extremely active and dangerous. Let man beware of it! I have heard only of one person who was stung by a copperhead in this country. The poor wretch instantly swelled in a most dreadful manner; a multitude of spots of different hues alternately appeared and vanished, on different parts of his body: his eyes were filled with madness and rage, he cast them on all present with the most vindictive looks: he thrust out his tongue as the snakes do; he hissed through his teeth with inconceivable strength, and became an object of terror to all bystanders. To the lividness of a corpse he united the desperate force of a maniac; they hardly were able to fasten him, so as to guard themselves from his attacks; when in the space of two hours death relieved the poor wretch from his struggles, and the spectators from their apprehensions. ...

One anecdote I must relate, the circumstances of which are as true as they are singular.[1] One of my constant walks when I am at leisure,

---

1 *singular* Unusual.

is in my lowlands, where I have the pleasure of seeing my cattle, horses, and colts. ... From this simple grove I have amused myself an hundred times in observing the great number of hummingbirds with which our country abounds: the wild blossoms everywhere attract the attention of these birds, which like bees subsist by suction. From this retreat I distinctly watch them in all their various attitudes; but their flight is so rapid that you cannot distinguish the motion of their wings. On this little bird nature has profusely lavished her most splendid colours; the most perfect azure, the most beautiful gold, the most dazzling red, are forever in contrast, and help to embellish the plumes of his majestic head. The richest pallet of the most luxuriant painter could never invent anything to be compared to the variegated tints with which this insect bird is arrayed. Its bill is as long and as sharp as a coarse sewing needle; like the bee, nature has taught it to find out in the calix of flowers and blossoms, those mellifluous[1] particles that serve it for sufficient food; and yet it seems to leave them untouched, undeprived of anything that our eyes can possibly distinguish. When it feeds, it appears as if immoveable, though continually on the wing; and sometimes, from what motives I know not, it will tear and lacerate flowers into a hundred pieces: for, strange to tell, they are the most irascible of the feathered tribe. Where do passions find room in so diminutive a body? They often fight with the fury of lions, until one of the combatants falls a sacrifice and dies. When fatigued, it has often perched within a few feet of me, and on such favourable opportunities I have surveyed it with the most minute attention. Its little eyes appear like diamonds, reflecting light on every side: most elegantly finished in all parts it is a miniature work of our great parent; who seems to have formed it the smallest, and at the same time the most beautiful of the winged species.

As I was one day sitting solitary and pensive in my primitive arbour, my attention was engaged by a strange sort of rustling noise at some paces distance. I looked all around without distinguishing anything, until I climbed one of my great hemp stalks; when to my astonishment, I beheld two snakes of considerable length, the one pursuing the other with great celerity through a hemp stubble field. The aggressor was of the black kind, six feet long; the fugitive was

---

1 *mellifluous* Honey-like.

a water snake, nearly of equal dimensions. They soon met, and in the fury of their first encounter, they appeared in an instant firmly twisted together; and whilst their united tails beat the ground, they mutually tried with open jaws to lacerate each other. What a fell aspect[1] did they present! Their heads were compressed to a very small size, their eyes flashed fire; and after this conflict had lasted about five minutes, the second found means to disengage itself from the first, and hurried toward the ditch. Its antagonist instantly assumed a new posture, and half creeping and half erect, with a majestic mien, overtook and attacked the other again, which placed itself in the same attitude, and prepared to resist. The scene was uncommon and beautiful, for thus opposed they fought with their jaws, biting each other with the utmost rage; but notwithstanding this appearance of mutual courage and fury, the water snake still seemed desirous of retreating toward the ditch, its natural element. This was no sooner perceived by the keen-eyed black one, than twisting its tail twice round a stalk of hemp, and seizing its adversary by the throat, not by means of its jaws, but by twisting its own neck twice round that of the water snake, pulled it back from the ditch. To prevent a defeat the latter took hold likewise of a stalk on the bank, and by the acquisition of that point of resistance became a match for its fierce antagonist. Strange was this to behold; two great snakes strongly adhering to the ground, mutually fastened together by means of the writhings which lashed them to each other, and stretched at their full length, they pulled but pulled in vain; and in the moments of greatest exertions that part of their bodies which was entwined, seemed extremely small, while the rest appeared inflated, and now and then convulsed with strong undulations, rapidly following each other. Their eyes seemed on fire, and ready to start out of their heads; at one time the conflict seemed decided; the water-snake bent itself into two great folds, and by that operation rendered the other more than commonly outstretched; the next minute the new struggles of the black one gained an unexpected superiority, it acquired two great folds likewise, which necessarily extended the body of its adversary in proportion as it had contracted its own. These efforts were alternate; victory seemed doubtful, inclining sometimes to the one side and sometimes to the other; until at last

---

1 *fell aspect* Dreadful appearance.

the stalk to which the black snake fastened, suddenly gave way, and in consequence of this accident they both plunged into the ditch. The water did not extinguish their vindictive rage; for by their agitations I could trace, though not distinguish, their mutual attacks. They soon re-appeared on the surface twisted together, as in their first onset; but the black snake seemed to retain its wonted[1] superiority, for its head was exactly fixed above that of the other, which it incessantly pressed down under the water, until it was stifled, and sunk. The victor no sooner perceived its enemy incapable of farther resistance, than abandoning it to the current, it returned on shore and disappeared.

from LETTER 12

DISTRESSES OF A FRONTIER MAN

I wish for a change of place; the hour is come at last, that I must fly from my house and abandon my farm! But what course shall I steer, enclosed as I am? The climate best adapted to my present situation and humour would be the polar regions, where six months day and six months night divide the dull year: nay, a simple Aurora Borealis would suffice me, and greatly refresh my eyes, fatigued now by so many disagreeable objects. The severity of those climates, that great gloom, where melancholy dwells, would be perfectly analogous to the turn of my mind. Oh, could I remove my plantation to the shores of the Oby, willingly would I dwell in the hut of a Samoyede; with cheerfulness would I go and bury myself in the cavern of a Laplander. Could I but carry my family along with me, I would winter at Pello, or Tobolsky, in order to enjoy the peace and innocence of that country.[2] But let me arrive under the pole, or reach the antipodes,[3] I never can leave behind me the remembrance of the dreadful scenes to which I have been a witness; therefore never can I be happy! Happy, why would I mention that sweet, that enchanting word? Once happiness was our portion; now it is gone from us, and I am afraid not to be enjoyed

---

1 *wonted* Usual.

2 *Oby ... that country* Crèvecoeur names numerous locations in far northern Europe; the Samoyedic people are an Indigenous group of Siberia (where the Oby River is located), while the Laplanders, or Sámi, are Indigenous peoples from parts of Norway, Sweden, and Finland.

3 *antipodes* I.e., the South Pole.

again by the present generation![1] Whichever way I look, nothing but the most frightful precipices present themselves to my view, in which hundreds of my friends and acquaintances have already perished: of all animals that live on the surface of this planet, what is man when no longer connected with society; or when he finds himself surrounded by a convulsed and a half dissolved one? He cannot live in solitude; he must belong to some community bound by some ties, however imperfect. Men mutually support and add to the boldness and confidence of each other; the weakness of each is strengthened by the force of the whole. I had never before these calamitous times formed any such ideas; I lived on, laboured and prospered, without having ever studied on what the security of my life, and the foundation of my prosperity were established: I perceived them just as they left me. Never was a situation so singularly terrible as mine, in every possible respect; as a member of an extensive society, as a citizen of an inferior division of the same society, as a husband, as a father, as a man who exquisitely feels for the miseries of others as well as for his own! But, alas! so much is everything now subverted among us, that the very word misery, with which we were hardly acquainted before, no longer conveys the same ideas; or rather tired with feeling for the miseries of others, everyone feels now for himself alone. When I consider myself as connected in all these characters, as bound by so many cords, all uniting in my heart, I am seized with a fever of the mind, I am transported beyond that degree of calmness which is necessary to delineate our thoughts. I feel as if my reason wanted to leave me, as if it would burst its poor weak tenement: again I try to compose myself, I grow cool, and preconceiving the dreadful loss, I endeavour to retain the useful guest.

You know the position of our settlement; I need not therefore describe it. To the west it is enclosed by a chain of mountains, reaching to ———; to the east, the country is as yet but thinly inhabited; we are almost insulated, and the houses are at a considerable distance from each other. From the mountains we have but too much reason to expect our dreadful enemy; the wilderness is a harbour where it is impossible to find them. It is a door through which they can enter

---

1   *not to be ... generation*   Letter 12 is written in the context of the onset of the American Revolutionary War.

our country whenever they please; and, as they seem determined to destroy the whole chain of frontiers, our fate cannot be far distant: from Lake Champlain, almost all has been conflagrated one after another. What renders these incursions still more terrible is, that they most commonly take place in the dead of the night: we never go to our fields but we are seized with an involuntary fear, which lessens our strength and weakens our labour. No other subject of conversation intervenes between the different accounts, which spread through the country, of successive acts of devastation; and these told in chimney-corners, swell themselves in our affrighted imaginations into the most terrific ideas! We never sit down either to dinner or supper, but the least noise immediately spreads a general alarm and prevents us from enjoying the comfort of our meals. The very appetite proceeding from labour and peace of mind is gone; we eat just enough to keep us alive: our sleep is disturbed by the most frightful dreams; sometimes I start awake, as if the great hour of danger was come; at other times the howling of our dogs seems to announce the arrival of the enemy: we leap out of bed and run to arms; my poor wife with panting bosom and silent tears, takes leave of me, as if we were to see each other no more; she snatches the youngest children from their beds, who, suddenly awakened, increase by their innocent questions the horror of the dreadful moment. She tries to hide them in the cellar, as if our cellar was inaccessible to the fire. I place all my servants at the windows, and myself at the door, where I am determined to perish. Fear industriously increases every sound; we all listen; each communicates to the other his ideas and conjectures. We remain thus sometimes for whole hours, our hearts and our minds racked by the most anxious suspense: what a dreadful situation, a thousand times worse than that of a soldier engaged in the midst of the most severe conflict! Sometimes feeling the spontaneous courage of a man, I seem to wish for the decisive minute; the next instant a message from my wife, sent by one of the children, puzzling me beside with their little questions, unmans me: away goes my courage, and I descend again into the deepest despondency. At last finding that it was a false alarm, we return once more to our beds; but what good can the kind sleep of nature do to us when interrupted by such scenes! Securely placed as you are, you can have no idea of our agitations but by hearsay; no relation can be equal to what we suffer and to what we feel. Every morning my youngest children are sure to have frightful dreams to relate: in vain I exert my authority to keep them silent. It is not in my power, and these images of their disturbed imagination, instead of being frivolously looked upon as in the days of our happiness, are on the contrary considered as warnings and sure prognostics of our future fate. I am not a superstitious man, but since our misfortunes, I am grown more timid, and less disposed to treat the doctrine of omens with contempt. ...

As a member of a large society which extends to many parts of the world, my connection with it is too distant to be as strong as that which binds me to the inferior division in the midst of which I live. I am told that the great nation of which we are a part[1] is just, wise, and free, beyond any other on earth, within its own insular boundaries; but not always so to its distant conquests: I shall not repeat all I have heard, because I cannot believe half of it. As a citizen of a smaller society, I find that any kind of opposition to its now prevailing sentiments immediately begets hatred: how easily do men pass from loving, to hating and cursing one another! I am a lover of peace; what must I do? I am divided between the respect I feel for the ancient connection,[2] and the fear of innovations, with the consequence of which I am not well acquainted; as they are embraced by my own countrymen. I am conscious that I was happy before this unfortunate Revolution. I feel that I am no longer so; therefore I regret the change. This is the only mode of reasoning adapted to persons in my situation. If I attach myself to the Mother Country, which is 3,000 miles from me, I become what is called an enemy to my own region; if I follow the rest of my countrymen, I become opposed to our ancient masters: both extremes appear equally dangerous to a person of so little weight and consequence as I am, whose energy and example are of no avail. As to the argument on which the dispute is founded, I know little about it. Much has been said and written on both sides, but who has a judgement capacious and clear enough to decide? The great moving principles which actuate both parties are much hid from vulgar eyes, like mine; nothing but the plausible and the probable are offered to our contemplation. The innocent class are

---

1   *great nation ... part*   I.e., Britain.
2   *ancient connection*   The tie between the American provinces and Britain.

always the victim of the few; they are in all countries and at all times the inferior agents, on which the popular phantom is erected; they clamour, and must toil, and bleed, and are always sure of meeting with oppression and rebuke. It is for the sake of the great leaders on both sides that so much blood must be spilt; that of the people is counted as nothing. Great events are not achieved for us, though it is *by* us that they are principally accomplished; by the arms, the sweat, the lives of the people. Books tell me so much that they inform me of nothing. Sophistry,[1] the bane of freemen, launches forth in all her deceiving attire! After all, most men reason from passions; and shall such an ignorant individual as I am decide, and say this side is right, that side is wrong? Sentiment and feeling are the only guides I know. Alas, how should I unravel an argument, in which reason herself hath given way to brutality and bloodshed! What then must I do? I ask the wisest lawyers, the ablest casuists,[2] the warmest patriots; for I mean honestly. Great Source of wisdom! inspire me with light sufficient to guide my benighted steps out of this intricate maze! Shall I discard all my ancient principles, shall I renounce that name, that nation which I held once so respectable? ... I cannot count the multitude of orphans this war has made; nor ascertain the immensity of blood we have lost. Some have asked whether it was a crime to resist; to repel some parts of this evil. Others have asserted that a resistance so general makes pardon unattainable, and repentance useless; and dividing the crime among so many, renders it imperceptible. What one party calls meritorious, the other denominates flagitious.[3] These opinions vary, contract, or expand, like the events of the war on which they are founded. What can an insignificant man do in the midst of these jarring contradictory parties, equally hostile to persons situated as I am? And after all who will be the really guilty? Those most certainly who fail of success. Our fate, the fate of thousands, is then necessarily involved in the dark wheel of fortune. Why then so many useless reasonings; we are the sport of fate. Farewell education, principles, love of our country, farewell; all are become useless to the generality of us: he who governs himself according to what he calls his principles, may be punished either by one party or the other, for

---

1   *Sophistry*   Deceptive reason or arguments.
2   *casuists*   Advisors on matters of duty and conscience.
3   *flagitious*   Criminal.

those very principles. He who proceeds without principle, as chance, timidity, or self-preservation directs, will not perhaps fare better; but he will be less blamed. What are *we* in the great scale of events, we poor defenseless frontier inhabitants? What is it to the gazing world, whether we breathe or whether we die? whatever virtue, whatever merit and disinterestedness we may exhibit in our secluded retreats, of what avail? ... I am informed that the king has the most numerous, as well as the fairest, progeny of children of any potentate now in the world:[1] he may be a great king, but he must feel as we common mortals do, in the good wishes he forms for their lives and prosperity. ... Oh! did he but know the circumstances of this horrid war, I am sure he would put a stop to that long destruction of parents and children. I am sure that while he turned his ears to state policy, he would attentively listen also to the dictates of nature, that great parent; for, as a good king, he no doubt wishes to create, to spare, and to protect, as she does. Must I then, in order to be called a faithful subject, coolly, and philosophically say, it is necessary for the good of Britain that my children's brains should be dashed against the walls of the house in which they were reared; that my wife should be stabbed and scalped before my face; that I should be either murdered or captivated; or that for greater expedition we should all be locked up and burnt to ashes as the family of the B——n was? ... No, it is impossible! so astonishing a sacrifice is not to be expected from human nature, it must belong to beings of an inferior or superior order, actuated by less, or by more refined principles. ...

Must I then bid farewell to Britain, to that renowned country? Must I renounce a name so ancient and so venerable? Alas, she herself, that once indulgent parent, forces me to take up arms against her. She herself, first inspired the most unhappy citizens of our remote districts, with the thoughts of shedding the blood of those whom they used to call by the name of friends and brethren. That great nation which now convulses the world; which hardly knows the extent of her Indian kingdoms; which looks toward the universal monarchy of trade, of industry, of riches, of power: why must she strew our poor frontiers with the carcasses of her friends, with the wrecks of our

---

1   *the king ... in the world*   King George III, who reigned from 1760 to 1820, had fifteen children with his wife, Queen Charlotte.

insignificant villages, in which there is no gold? When, oppressed by painful recollection, I revolve all these scattered ideas in my mind; when I contemplate my situation, and the thousand streams of evil with which I am surrounded; when I descend into the particular tendency even of the remedy I have proposed, I am convulsed—convulsed sometimes to that degree, as to be tempted to exclaim—Why has the master of the world permitted so much indiscriminate evil throughout every part of this poor planet, at all times, and among all kinds of people? It ought surely to be the punishment of the wicked only. I bring that cup to my lips, of which I must soon taste, and shudder at its bitterness. What then is life, I ask myself, is it a gracious gift? No, it is too bitter; a gift means something valuable conferred, but life appears to be a mere accident, and of the worst kind: we are born to be victims of diseases and passions, of mischances and death: better not to be than to be miserable. Thus impiously I roam, I fly from one erratic thought to another, and my mind, irritated by these acrimonious reflections, is ready sometimes to lead me to dangerous extremes of violence. When I recollect that I am a father, and a husband, the return of these endearing ideas strikes deep into my heart. Alas! they once made it to glow with pleasure and with every ravishing exultation; but now they fill it with sorrow. At other times, my wife industriously rouses me out of these dreadful meditations, and soothes me by all the reasoning she is mistress of; but her endeavours only serve to make me more miserable, by reflecting that she must share with all these calamities, the bare apprehensions of which I am afraid will subvert her reason. Nor can I with patience think that a beloved wife, my faithful helpmate throughout all my rural schemes, the principal hand which has assisted me in rearing the prosperous fabric of ease and independence I lately possessed, as well as my children, those tenants of my heart, should daily and nightly be exposed to such a cruel fate. Self-preservation is above all political precepts and rules, and even superior to the dearest opinions of our minds; a reasonable accommodation of ourselves to the various exigencies of the time in which we live, is the most irresistible precept. To this great evil I must seek some sort of remedy adapted to remove or to palliate it; situated as I am, what steps should I take that will neither injure nor insult any of the parties, and at the same time save my family from that certain destruction which awaits it, if I remain here much longer. Could I ensure them bread, safety, and subsistence, not the bread of idleness, but that earned by proper labour as heretofore; could this be accomplished by the sacrifice of my life, I would willingly give it up. I attest before heaven, that it is only for these I would wish to live and to toil: for these whom I have brought into this miserable existence. I resemble, methinks, one of the stones of a ruined arch, still retaining that pristine form which anciently fitted the place I occupied, but the centre is tumbled down; I can be nothing until I am replaced, either in the former circle, or in some stronger one. I see one on a smaller scale, and at a considerable distance, but it is within my power to reach it: and since I have ceased to consider myself as a member of the ancient state now convulsed, I willingly descend into an inferior one. I will revert into a state approaching nearer to that of nature, unencumbered either with voluminous laws, or contradictory codes, often galling the very necks, of those whom they protect; and at the same time sufficiently remote from the brutality of unconnected savage nature. Do you, my friend, perceive the path I have found out? it is that which leads to the tenants of the great —— village of ——, where, far removed from the accursed neighbourhood of Europeans, its inhabitants live with more ease, decency, and peace, than you imagine: where, though governed by no laws, yet find, in uncontaminated simple manners all that laws can afford. Their system is sufficiently complete to answer all the primary wants of man, and to constitute him a social being, such as he ought to be in the great forest of nature. There it is that I have resolved at any rate to transport myself and my family: an eccentric thought, you may say, thus to cut asunder all former connections, and to form new ones with a people whom nature has stamped with such different characteristics! But as the happiness of my family is the only object of my wishes, I care very little where we be, or where we go, provided that we are safe, and all united together. ... It is not, believe me, a disappointed ambition which leads me to take this step, it is the bitterness of my situation, it is the impossibility of knowing what better measure to adopt: my education fitted me for nothing more than the most simple occupations of life; I am but a feller of trees, a cultivator of land, the most honourable title an American can have. I have no exploits, no discoveries, no inventions to boast of; I have cleared about 370 acres of land, some for the plough, some for the scythe; and this has occupied many years of my life. I have never possessed, or wish to possess anything more than what could be earned or produced by the united industry of my family. I wanted nothing more than to live at home independent and tranquil, and to teach my children how to provide the means of a future ample subsistence, founded on labour, like that of their father. This is the career of life I have pursued, and that which I had marked out for them and for which they seemed to be so well calculated by their inclinations, and by their constitutions. But now these pleasing expectations are gone, we must abandon the accumulated industry of nineteen years, we must fly we hardly know whither, through the most impervious paths, and become members of a new and strange community. ... I have at all times generously relieved what few distressed people I have met with; I have encouraged the industrious; my house has always been opened to travellers; I have not lost a month in illness since I have been a man; I have caused upwards of an hundred and twenty families to remove hither. Many of them I have led by the hand in the days of their first trial; distant as I am from any places of worship or school of education, I have been the pastor of my family, and the teacher of many of my neighbours. I have learnt[1] them as well as I could the gratitude they owe to God, the father of harvests; and their duties to man: I have been as useful a subject; ever obedient to the laws, ever vigilant to see them respected and observed. My wife hath faithfully followed the same line within her province; no woman was ever a better economist,[2] or spun or wove better linen. Yet we must perish, perish like wild beasts, included within a ring of fire!

Yes, I will cheerfully embrace that resource; it is an holy inspiration. By night and by day, it presents itself to my mind: I have carefully revolved the scheme;[3] I have considered in all its future effects and tendencies, the new mode of living we must pursue, without salt, without spices, without linen and with little other clothing; the art of hunting we must acquire; the new manners we must adopt; the new language we must speak; the dangers attending the education of my children we must endure. These changes may appear more terrific at a distance perhaps than when grown familiar by practice: what is it

---

1   *learnt*   Taught.
2   *economist*   I.e., manager of household tasks and finances.
3   *revolved the scheme*   Turned the plan over in my mind.

to us, whether we eat well made pastry, or pounded àlagrichés;[1] well roasted beef, or smoked venison; cabbages, or squashes? Whether we wear neat home-spun, or good beaver; whether we sleep on feather-beds, or on bear-skins? The difference is not worth attending to. The difficulty of the language, the fear of some great intoxication among the Indians; finally, the apprehension lest my younger children should be caught by that singular charm, so dangerous at their tender years; are the only considerations that startle me. By what power does it come to pass, that children who have been adopted when young among these people, can never be prevailed on to re-adopt European manners? Many an anxious parent I have seen last war,[2] who at the return of the peace, went to the Indian villages where they knew their children had been carried in captivity; when to their inexpressible sorrow, they found them so perfectly Indianised, that many knew them no longer, and those whose more advanced ages permitted them to recollect their fathers and mothers, absolutely refused to follow them, and ran to their adopted parents for protection against the effusions of love their unhappy real parents lavished on them! Incredible as this may appear, I have heard it asserted in a thousand instances, among persons of credit. In the village of ——, where I purpose to go, there lived, about fifteen years ago, an Englishman and a Swede, whose history would appear moving, had I time to relate it. They were grown to the age of men when they were taken; they happily escaped the great punishment of war captives, and were obliged to marry the *squaws*[3] who had saved their lives by adoption. By the force of habit, they became at last thoroughly naturalised to this wild course of life. While I was there, their friends sent them a considerable sum of money to ransom themselves with. The Indians, their old masters, gave them their choice, and without requiring any consideration, told them that they had been long as free as themselves. They chose to remain; and the reasons they gave me would greatly surprise you: the most perfect freedom, the ease of living, the absence of those cares and corroding solicitudes which so often prevail with us; the peculiar goodness of

---

1   *pounded àlagrichés*   Dishes of corn kernel mush.
2   *last war*   During the previous war (the Seven Years' War, 1756–63).
3   *squaws*   Now considered indisputably offensive, this term for Indigenous women likely has roots in the Massachusett and other Algonquian languages; in Crèvecoeur's time it was still often intended as a neutral term, though derogatory connotations had certainly arisen.

the soil they cultivated, for they did not trust altogether to hunting; all these, and many more motives, which I have forgot, made them prefer that life, of which we entertain such dreadful opinions. It cannot be, therefore, so bad as we generally conceive it to be; there must be in their social bond something singularly captivating, and far superior to anything to be boasted of among us; for thousands of Europeans are Indians, and we have no examples of even one of those Aborigines having from choice become Europeans! ... In my youth I traded with the ———, under the conduct of my uncle, and always traded justly and equitably; some of them remember it to this day. Happily their village is far removed from the dangerous neighbourhood of the whites; I sent a man last spring to it, who understands the woods extremely well, and who speaks their language; he is just returned, after several weeks absence, and has brought me, as I had flattered myself, a string of thirty purple wampum,[1] as a token that their honest chief will spare us half of his wigwam until we have time to erect one. He has sent me word that they have land in plenty, of which they are not so covetous as the whites; that we may plant for ourselves, and that in the meantime he will procure us some corn and some meat; that fish is plenty in the waters of ———, and that the village to which he had laid open my proposals, have no objection to our becoming dwellers with them. I have not yet communicated these glad tidings to my wife, nor do I know how to do it; I tremble lest she should refuse to follow me; lest the sudden idea of this removal rushing on her mind, might be too powerful. I flatter myself I shall be able to accomplish it, and to prevail on her; I fear nothing but the effects of her strong attachment to her relations. I would willingly let you know how I purpose to remove my family to so great a distance, but it would become unintelligible to you, because you are not acquainted with the geographical situation of this part of the country. Suffice it for you to know, that with about twenty-three miles land carriage,[2] I am enabled to perform the rest by water; and when once afloat, I care not whether it be two or three hundred miles. I propose to send all our provisions, furniture, and clothes to my wife's father, who approves of the scheme, and to reserve nothing but a few necessary

---

1 *wampum*   Shell beads used by various Indigenous peoples for purposes including record-keeping and trade.
2 *land carriage*   Of overland travel.

articles of covering; trusting to the furs of the chase, for our future apparel. Were we imprudently to encumber ourselves too much with baggage, we should never reach to the waters of ———, which is the most dangerous as well as the most difficult part of our journey; and yet but a trifle in point of distance. I intend to say to my negroes—In the name of God, be free, my honest lads, I thank you for your past services; go, from henceforth, and work for yourselves; look on me as your old friend, and fellow labourer; be sober, frugal, and industrious, and you need not fear earning a comfortable subsistence. Lest my countrymen should think that I am gone to join the incendiaries of our frontiers, I intend to write a letter to Mr. ———, to inform him of our retreat, and of the reasons that have urged me to it. The man whom I sent to ——— village, is to accompany us also, and a very useful companion he will be on every account.

You may therefore, by means of anticipation, behold me under the wigwam; I am so well acquainted with the principal manners of these people, that I entertain not the least apprehension from them. I rely more securely on their strong hospitality, than on the witnessed compacts of many Europeans. As soon as possible after my arrival, I design to build myself a wigwam, after the same manner and size with the rest, in order to avoid being thought singular, or giving occasion for any railleries;[1] though these people are seldom guilty of such European follies. I shall erect it hard by[2] the lands which they propose to allot me, and will endeavour that my wife, my children, and myself may be adopted soon after our arrival. Thus becoming truly inhabitants of their village, we shall immediately occupy that rank within the pale[3] of their society, which will afford us all the amends we can possibly expect for the loss we have met with by the convulsions of our own. According to their customs we shall likewise receive names from them, by which we shall always be known. My youngest children shall learn to swim, and to shoot with the bow, that they may acquire such talents as will necessarily raise them into some degree of esteem among the Indian lads of their own age; the rest of us must hunt with the hunters. I have been for several years an expert marksman; but I dread lest the imperceptible charm of Indian education may seize my

---

1 *railleries* Mockeries.
2 *hard by* Close to.
3 *pale* Boundaries.

younger children, and give them such a propensity to that mode of life as may preclude their returning to the manners and customs of their parents. I have but one remedy to prevent this great evil; and that is, to employ them in the labour of the fields, as much as I can; I am even resolved to make their daily subsistence depend altogether on it. As long as we keep ourselves busy in tilling the earth, there is no fear of any of us becoming wild; it is the chase and the food it procures that have this strange effect. Excuse a simile—those hogs which range in the woods, and to whom grain is given once a week, preserve their former degree of tameness; but if, on the contrary, they are reduced to live on ground nuts, and on what they can get, they soon become wild and fierce. For my part, I can plough, sow, and hunt, as occasion m[a]y require; but my wife, deprived of wool and flax, will have no room for industry; what is she then to do? Like the other squaws, she must cook for us the nasaump, the ninchickè, and such other preparations of corn as are customary among these people. She must learn to bake squashes and pumkins under the ashes; to slice and smoke the meat of our own killing, in order to preserve it; she must chearfully adopt the manners and customs of her neighbours, in their dress, deportment, conduct, and internal economy—in all respects. Surely if we can have fortitude enough to quit all we have, to remove so far, and to associate with people so different from us, these necessary compliances are but subordinate parts of the scheme. The change of garments, when those they carry with them are worn out, will not be the least of my wife's and daughter's concerns, though I am in hopes that self-love will invent some sort of reparation. Perhaps you would not believe that there are in the woods looking-glasses, and paint of every colour; and that the inhabitants take as much pains to adorn their faces and their bodies, to fix their bracelets of silver, and plait their hair, as our forefathers the Picts[1] used to do in the time of the Romans. Not that I would wish to see either my wife or daughter adopt those savage customs; we can live in great peace and harmony with them without descending to every article; the interruption of trade hath, I hope, suspended this mode of dress.

---

1   *Picts*   Ancient Celtic people, native to what is now Scotland; Picts were often described as adorning themselves with elaborate blue tattoos, though there is little historical evidence for this idea.

My wife understands inoculation perfectly well,[1] she inoculated all our children one after another, and has successfully performed that operation on several scores of people, who, scattered here and there through our woods, were too far removed from all medical assistance. If we can persuade but one family to submit to it, and it succeeds, we shall then be as happy as our situation will admit of; it will raise her into some degree of consideration, for whoever is useful in any society will always be respected. If we are so fortunate as to carry one family through a disorder, which is the plague among these people, I trust to the force of example, we shall then become truly necessary, valued, and beloved: we indeed owe every kind office to a society of men who so readily offer to admit us into their social partnership, and to extend to my family the shelter of their village, the strength of their adoption, and even the dignity of their names. God grant us a prosperous beginning, we may then hope to be of more service to them than even missionaries who have been sent to preach to them a Gospel they cannot understand.

As to religion, our mode of worship will not suffer much by this removal from a cultivated country, into the bosom of the woods; for it cannot be much simpler than that which we have followed here these many years: and I will with as much care as I can, redouble my attention, and twice a week retrace to them the great outlines of their duty to God and to man. I will read and expound to them some part of the decalogue, which is the method I have pursued ever since I married. ...

... Thus shall we metamorphose ourselves, from neat, decent, opulent planters, surrounded with every conveniency which our external labour and internal industry could give, into a still simpler people divested of everything beside hope, food, and the raiment of the woods: abandoning the large framed house, to dwell under the wigwam; and the featherbed, to lie on the matt, or bear's skin. There shall we sleep undisturbed by fruitful dreams and apprehensions; rest and peace of mind will make us the most ample amends for what we shall leave behind[.] These blessings cannot be purchased too dear; too long have we been deprived of them. I would cheerfully go even

---

1   *understands ... well* Inoculation against smallpox was introduced into Britain in the early eighteenth century; it was first practiced in America around 1720.

to the Missisippi, to find that repose to which we have been so long strangers. My heart sometimes seems tired with beating, it wants rest like my eyelids, which feel oppressed with so many watchings.

These are the component parts of my scheme, the success of each of which appears feasible; from whence I flatter myself with the probable success of the whole. ...

Thus then in the village of ——, in the bosom of that peace it has enjoyed ever since I have known it, connected with mild hospitable people, strangers to *our* political disputes, and having none among themselves; on the shores of a fine river, surrounded with woods, abounding with game; our little society united in perfect harmony with the new adoptive one, in which we shall be incorporated, shall rest I hope from all fatigues, from all apprehensions, from our present terrors, and from our long watchings. Not a word of politics shall cloud our simple conversation; tired either with the chase or the labour of the field, we shall sleep on our mats without any distressing want, having learnt to retrench every superfluous one: we shall have but two prayers to make to the Supreme Being—that he may shed his fertilizing dew on our little crops, and that he will be pleased to restore peace to our unhappy country. These shall be the only subject of our nightly prayers, and of our daily ejaculations:[1] and if the labour, the industry, the frugality, the union of men can be an agreeable offering to him, we shall not fail to receive his paternal blessings. There I shall contemplate nature in her most wild and ample extent; I shall carefully study a species of society of which I have at present but very imperfect ideas; I will endeavour to occupy with propriety that place which will enable me to enjoy the few and sufficient benefits it confers. The solitary and unconnected mode of life I have lived in my youth must fit me for this trial, I am not the first who has attempted it; Europeans did not, it is true, carry to the wilderness numerous families; they went there as mere speculators; I, as a man seeking a refuge from the desolation of war. They went there to study the manners of the aborigines; I to conform to them, whatever they are. Some went as visitors, as travellers; I as a sojourner, as a fellow hunter and labourer, go determined industriously to work up among them such a system of happiness as may be adequate to my future situation,

---

1   *ejaculations*   Passionately spoken words.

and may be a sufficient compensation for all my fatigues and for the misfortunes I have borne. I have always found it at home; I may hope likewise to find it under the humble roof of my wigwam.

O! Supreme Being, if among the immense variety of planets, inhabited by thy creative power, thy paternal and omnipotent care deigns to extend to all the individuals they contain; if it be not beneath thy infinite dignity to cast thy eyes on us wretched mortals; if my future felicity is not contrary to the necessary effects of those secret causes which thou hast appointed, receive the supplications of a man to whom in thy kindness thou hast given a wife and an offspring: View us all with benignity, sanctify this strong conflict of regrets, wishes, and other natural passions; guide our steps through these unknown paths, and bless our future mode of life. If it is good and well meant, it must proceed from thee; thou knowest, O Lord, our enterprise contains neither fraud, nor malice, nor revenge. Bestow on me that energy of conduct now become so necessary, that it may be in my power to carry the young family thou hast given me through this great trial with safety and in thy peace. ... Permit, I beseech thee, O Father of nature, that our ancient virtues, and our industry, may not be totally lost: and that as a reward for the great toils we have made on this new land we may be restored to our ancient tranquility, and enabled to fill it with successive generations, that will constantly thank thee for the ample subsistence thou hast given them.

The unreserved manner in which I have written must give you a convincing proof of that friendship and esteem of which I am sure you never yet doubted. As members of the same society, as mutually bound by the ties of affection and old acquaintance, you certainly cannot avoid feeling for my distresses; you cannot avoid mourning with me over that load of physical and moral evil with which we are all oppressed. My own share of it I often overlook when I minutely contemplate all that hath befallen our native country.

FINIS

—1782

In Context

A Pennsylvania Farm

Though the farm Crèvecoeur himself purchased was in Orange Country, New York, his Farmer James inherits a large farm in Pennsylvania—"three hundred and seventy-one acres of land," as he describes
it in Letter 2. We do not have a detailed visual record of any very
similar farm in Pennsylvania in the 1770s; one interesting point of
comparison, though, is Belfield, a Pennsylvania property purchased
by Charles Willson Peale in 1800. Peale—now known primarily as
an artist but at the time renowned for his accomplishments in a wide
range of fields—added ornamental features to some of the property,
but also maintained it as a large working farm. Belfield Farm occupied
104 acres—considerably smaller than Farmer James's, but still a very
substantial property.

Charles Willson Peale, Belfield Farm, c. 1816 (Detroit Institute of Arts).

Charles Willson Peale, *Cabbage Patch, The Gardens of Belfield*, Pennsylvania, c. 1816 (Pennsylvania Academy of the Fine Arts).

Nantucket and Charles-Town

Nantucket and its environs and Charles-Town and its environs present contrasting faces of America to Crèvecoeur's Farmer James. Images of both are provided here.

"The inhabitants are the gayest in America; [Charles-Town] is called the centre of our beau monde," wrote Crèvecoeur in the late eighteenth century. Many of the buildings from that era are still standing—including the building now known as "the Pink House," which dates from 1712 and which served as a tavern for much of the eighteenth century. Photograph by Brian Stansberry, 2010 (licensed under CC BY 3.0.).

The Town of Sherbourne on the Island of Nantucket, 1775.

Indigo Processing, St. Stephen's Parish [approximately 30 miles north of Charlestown], 1762.

Reactions to *Letters from an American Farmer*

As the introduction to this volume suggests, the reception history of *Letters from an American Farmer* is of considerable interest. Included here are three documents from that history. The first was published as a 26-page pamphlet in London. How well it sold is not clear, but it may well have enjoyed a wide circulation; the *Newcastle Chronicle*, the *Derby Mercury*, and the *Bath Chronicle* were among the many newspapers in which the pamphlet was advertised in February 1783. The second—a book review—appeared in a prestigious French publication not long after the French edition of Crèvecoeur's work was issued; the third appeared in a popular 1900 history of American literature.

from Rev. Samuel Ayscough, *Remarks on the* Letters from an American Farmer; *or, a Detection of the Errors of Mr. J. Hector Saint John; Pointing out the Pernicious Tendency of Those Letters to Great Britain* (1783)

At a time like the present, when the weight of accumulated taxes, the natural consequence of war, will create a dissatisfaction in the minds of many persons with their situations, and make them ready to look out for a settlement in a country where they may hope to obtain a mutual defence with a less expense of government. ...

If care be not taken ..., we shall have the mortification of beholding our inhabitants flocking to that country, which has lately imbrued its fields with the blood of many thousands of our unhappy countrymen; that country which has been some years the seat of horrid war; that country which has become depopulated, its villages deserted, and its fields unfruitful through want of cultivation.

The time being come when the independence of America is in some measure acknowledged by this country, we already see allurements thrown out to encourage the inhabitants of all nations to come and settle with them, and by that means to recover their country from the desolation it has sustained by the war, by draining various nations of their most useful inhabitants, without waiting for the slow increase of natural population. ... As false lights are already held out to impose on the credulous, it is the duty of every good citizen to draw aside the veil under which truth is eclipsed.

For these reasons I am induced to lay my sentiments before the public in a most candid and dispassionate manner, anxious to expose an attempt of a late[1] author to mislead the people, and to show that the publication is a fraud, artfully disguised, and hostile to the happiness of the nation. ...

The pleasing, romantic manner in which the letters, said to be the production of an American farmer, are written, is calculated to work upon the passions, and has gained them a credit in the world, which will be with difficulty effaced by a dry writer of mere facts. The pen of this writer would make an Irish hut appear a palace[.] ...

In this manner the wretched inhabitants of the barren islands of Nantucket and Martha's Vineyard become the envy of those who enjoy every blessing which Nature kindly grants. ...

The author, at p. 212, calls America his native country; and in several places boasts of his paternal estate; whilst it is a fact well known that he is a Frenchman, born in Normandy; that his residence was chiefly at New York, and there looked upon by the Loyalists as no friend to Englishmen.

To prove [that] this author was not a farmer, I shall examine the internal evidence of the Letters. ...

The author describes himself "as a simple cultivator of the earth, who had no other education than reading and writing." ... A simple cultivator of the earth ought to have told a plain tale, without the brilliancy of imagination, or the ornament of figures.[2] But these letters discover[3] the characteristic declamation of the Frenchman, the frothy metaphors of the rhetorician, and the distinguishing verbiage of the petty philosopher of France.

If we enquire into the facts asserted in this book, we find ample room for doubt. ...

... He then proceeds in giving a commonplace account of negro slavery; but our author is very unhappy in introducing something which must render the credit of the whole doubtful. In this predicament is the story of a slave suspended in an iron cage; it is related in an affecting manner, but he forgot that, although the punishment is sometimes inflicted, it is always by the side of a public road, and not in a solitary grove. ...

---

1   *late*   Recent.
2   *figures*   Fantastical or imaginary images.
3   *discover*   Reveal.

If we turn our attention to the object[1] of the book, it will plainly appear to be designed for the purpose of encouraging foreigners to emigrate and settle in America. ...

As another motive of encouragement to the abandoned and dissolute to seek their fortune in America, our author holds out the total want[2] of religion, that coming amongst others like themselves, they may pursue their wicked courses, and live without God in this world, or without the dread of him in a future. Thus, by all means, he hopes to gain fame.

This shows the necessity of an established church, without which a total forgetfulness of all religion necessarily takes place. ...

It was a prejudice unworthy of a philosophical farmer to remark, p. 51, "That the province of Nova Scotia is very thinly inhabited; that the power of the crown, in conjunction with the mosquitoes, had prevented men from settling there. Yet some parts of it flourished once, and it contained a mild, harmless set of people." Our farmer, who is fond of making reflections on nature and nature's laws, and doubtless being a judge of the fertility of the country, might have discovered, had the recital of truth been his object, that the barrenness of the soil, and fogginess of the atmosphere, had been at all times the real obstructions to the population of a country which, though it has been praised by philosophers, has always been avoided by settlers.

It is unnecessary for me to add anything more on this subject, having, as I think, shown sufficiently the credit which this book merits, and shall beg leave to remind the censors of literary productions that they ought to be more careful of recommending books composed of so many falsities, and fraught with such a fatal tendency. ...

To check as much as possible the fatal tendency of such publications cannot be an object beneath the attention of the guardians of our laws and liberties; and no method is more salutary than by making such wise laws, and giving such encouragement to our agriculture, manufactures, and commerce, as shall provide sufficient resources for employing the industry of all our people, and enabling them to live

---

1 *object* Goal; purpose.
2 *want* Lack.

contented with their condition, without wishing to pursue romantic schemes, for the attainment of that happiness which they might enjoy at home, under the mildest of governments and the best of kings.

from *Correspondance Littéraire, Philosophique et Critique par Grimm, Diderot, Raynal, Meister, etc.*[1] (January 1785)

The author of this work is named M. de Crèvecœur; he is a gentleman from Normandy who has spent twenty-four years of his life in North America, to which he just returned with the title of French Consul in New York. He had first written his work in English, and it is he himself who has just translated it into French.

This book, written without method and without art, but with much interest and sensitivity, perfectly fulfills the purpose that the author seems to have proposed, that is, to make one love America and all the advantages attached to the soil, to the constitution, and to the customs of the thirteen United Provinces. There are some minute details, some very common truths, some repetitions and some tedious parts; but it attaches by simple and true depictions, by the expression of an honest soul, profoundly penetrated by the feeling of all the domestic virtues, by all the happiness that is available to a man, a sweet independence, diligent work, the attachment of a dear family, the pleasure of a secure and legitimate property.

While waiting for half of Europe to become a province of America, as it may be destined to become one day, it seems to me that, if I were king, with the best intention of making my subjects happy and never constraining their freedom, this would be one of the books that I would be the most tempted to defend reading. There is hardly another that can be more suitable for encouraging the sort of emigration to which our Europeans already appear only too disposed. Over the past year the new republic saw further growth of its population from eleven to twelve thousand emigrants, most of whom were Scots and Germans; it's a fact we have from the very mouth of M. Franklin.[2]

---

1   *from Correspondance Littéraire ... etc.*   Translation by Genevieve Kirk, revised by Helena Snopek, copyright © Broadview Press.

2   *M. Franklin*   Benjamin Franklin (1706–90).

Some of the author's remarks on the condition and the character of the savages would have enraptured J.J. Rousseau;[1] he would have learned with delight that several children kidnapped during the war by the savages, reclaimed during peacetime by their parents, absolutely refused to follow them, and took refuge under the protection of their new friends, to escape the outpouring of paternal love; some others, since their return, do not cease to moan over the loss they endured, and never speak of it without shedding tears of grief.

Then continue to refuse to believe, if you dare, that the natural state of man is not civilization.

from Barrett Wendell, *A Literary History of America* (1900)

The political pamphlets of revolutionary America, of course, like the impassioned outbursts of Otis and of Patrick Henry[2] and of the other orators whose names are preserved in our manuals of patriotic elocution, were phrased in the style of the eighteenth century. Whatever their phrasing, these pamphlets indicate in our country a kind of intellectual activity which in England had displayed itself most characteristically a hundred years earlier. More and more, one begins to think, the secret of the American Revolution may be found in the fact that while under the influence of European conditions the English temperament had steadily altered from that of spontaneous, enthusiastic, versatile Elizabethans to that of stubborn, robust John Bull,[3] the original American temper, born under Elizabeth herself, had never deeply changed.

What the difference was, to be sure, may long remain a matter of dispute; but before the end of the eighteenth century, native Americans[4] had begun to feel it. Francis Hopkinson, a remarkably vivacious

---

1   *J.J. Rousseau*   Jean-Jacques Rousseau (1712–78), French philosopher who wrote extensively on the "state of nature"—often understood by Europeans to be comparable to the form of society in which various Indigenous peoples lived—as being the natural and most favorable state of humankind.
2   *Otis*   Mercy Otis Warren (1728–1814), political writer who passionately condemned the colonial regime in America;   *Patrick Henry*   Celebrated orator and American Founder (1736–99), best known for his impassioned speech, "Give me liberty, or give me death!"
3   *John Bull*   Personification of England originating in the early 1700s, generally as a stout, middle-aged man, conservative and matter-of-fact in personality.
4   *native Americans*   I.e., people of European ancestry but born in the Americas.

and spirited writer, was among the first to specify the fact. A Philadelphia gentleman born in 1737, he saw something of a good society in England between 1766 and 1768. He was a signer of the Declaration of Independence; and he died United States District Judge for Pennsylvania in 1792. His only familiar work is his satirical poem, "The Battle of the Kegs," but his writings in general are entertaining; and in the posthumous collection of his works is a passage, apparently written during the revolutionary period, which shows beyond question that he felt as distinctly as people feel today how different the temperaments of England and of America had become:

This infatuated [English] people have wearied the world for these hundred years with loud eulogiums upon liberty and their constitution; and yet they see that constitution languishing in a deep decay without making any effort for its recovery. Amused with trifles, and accustomed to venality[1] and corruption, they are not alarmed at the consequences of their supineness.[2] They love to talk of their glorious constitution because the idea is agreeable, and they are satisfied with the idea; and they honour their king, because it is the fashion to honour the king. ...

The extreme ignorance of the common people ... can scarce be credited. In general, they know nothing beyond the particular branch of business which their parents or the parish happened to choose for them. This, indeed, they practise with unremitting diligence; but never think of extending their knowledge farther.

A manufacturer has been brought up a maker of pin-heads; he has been at this business forty years and, of course, makes pin-heads with great dexterity; but he cannot make a whole pin for his life. He thinks it is the perfection of human nature to make pin-heads. He leaves other matters to inferior abilities. ...

In America, the lowest tradesman ... is not without some degree of general knowledge. They turn their heads to everything; their situation obliges them to do so. A farmer there cannot run to an artist[3] upon every trifling occasion. He must make and mend and contrive for himself. This I observed in my travels through the country. In many towns and in every city, they have public libraries. Not a tradesman

---

1   *venality*   The state of being overly mercenary—too willing to act for the sake of financial or other worldly rewards.
2   *supineness*   Laziness.
3   *artist*   Artisan; i.e., someone who can "make and mend and contrive" things.

but will find time to read. He acquires knowledge imperceptibly. He is amused with voyages and travels and becomes acquainted with the geography, customs, and commerce of other countries. He reads political disquisitions and learns the great outlines of his rights as a man and a citizen. He dips a little into philosophy and knows that the apparent motion of the sun is occasioned by the real motion of the earth. In a word, he is sure that, notwithstanding the determination of the king, lords, and commons to the contrary, two and two can never make five.

Such are the people of England, and such the people of America.

It is worthwhile to compare with this sketch of Hopkinson's a passage concerning Americans written a little later by a Frenchman, named Crèvecœur, who resided near New York from 1754 to 1780:

> ... The American is a new man, who acts upon new principles; he must therefore entertain new ideas, and form new opinions. From involuntary idleness, servile dependence, penury, and useless labour, he has passed to toils of a very different nature, rewarded by ample subsistence. This is an American.

The contrast between these two passages is sharp. Hopkinson's American is, after all, a human being; Crèvecœur's American is no more human than some ideal savage of Voltaire.[1] And yet, in Crèvecœur's time and since, it has been the fashion to suppose that the French understand us better than our true brothers, the English.

For this there is a certain ground. Englishmen are not accessible to general ideas, and they are not explosive. The French are both; and so, like the subjects of Queen Elizabeth, are the native Americans. Since 1775, then, America has often seemed more nearly at one with France than with England. Suggestive evidence of a deeper truth may be found in the career of the national hero whom the French cherish in common with ourselves—Lafayette.[2] Stirred by enthusiasm for the rights of man, he offered his sword to those rebellious colonies whom

---

1 *Voltaire* French philosopher (1694–1778). The figure of the "ideal" or "noble savage" was frequently discussed in French Enlightenment philosophy, representing humanity in a hypothetical and idealized "state of nature."

2 *Lafayette* Gilbert du Motier, Marquis de Lafayette (1757–1834), French-born military officer who became celebrated in the United States and France for his leading roles in both the American and French revolutions.

he believed to be fighting for mere abstract principles; and he had war-
rant for his belief, in the glittering generalities of the Declaration of
Independence. He saw our Revolution triumphant. He went back to
France, and saw the Revolution there end in tragic failure. To the last
he could never guess why the abstract principles which had worked
so admirably in America would not work in France. The real truth
he never perceived. Whatever reasons the revolutionary Americans
gave for their conduct, their underlying impulse was one which they
had inherited unchanged from their immigrant ancestors; namely,
that the rights for which men should die are not abstract but legal.
The abstract phrases of American thought remain superficial. By 1775,
however, the course of American history had made our conception
of legal rights different from that of the English. We had developed
local traditions of our own, which we believed as immemorial as ever
were the local traditions of the mother country. The question of rep-
resentation, for example, was not abstract; it was one of established
constitutional practice; but when we came to discussing it, we did not
understand each other's terms. Misunderstanding followed, a family
quarrel, a civil war, and world disunion. Beneath this world disunion,
all the while, is a deeper fact, binding American and England at last
together at heart—each really and truly believed itself to be asserting
the rights which immemorial custom had sanctioned. Revolutionary
France, on the other hand, tried to introduce into human history a
system of abstract rights different from anything which ever flourished under the sun.

Rationalizing Colonialism: Thomas Hobbes, John Locke, and George Washington

Many of the ideas expressed in Crèvecoeur's *Letters from an American Farmer*—the emphasis on land ownership, the espousal of values such as industriousness and productivity, and the accounts of Native American society and history (found especially in Letter 4)—are informed significantly by the social contract and state-of-nature theories examined by English philosophers such as Thomas Hobbes (1588–1679) and John Locke (1632–1704) in the preceding century. Hobbes's influential book *Leviathan* was the first significant European text to describe a theoretical "natural condition of mankind"—a state in which people live without government and without any agreed-upon laws aside from certain instinctively evident principles—and Hobbes asserted somewhat controversially that the state of nature was necessarily also a state of conflict. Building on this foundation, though with several important differences, John Locke set out in his *Second Treatise on Civil Government* his theory as to how the idea of personal property arises out of the state of nature, and how legitimate civil government arises out of a social need to protect that property. Both authors frequently invoked conceptions of Native American society as examples of the so-called state of nature.

Locke's work in particular would have a profound influence on European colonizers; many drew on Locke in attempting to justify their taking possession of Native American land in the eighteenth and nineteenth centuries. He frequently contrasts those whose claim to property rests on the "improvement of labor" they have provided with those who may have occupied the land but have not made it productive through labor. He also goes on to introduce the idea of money as a fair replacement for one's own labor, and suggests that the labor of those one has hired can in fact be counted as one's own labor. For Locke, issues of property were as much a real practical concern in America as they were in England, where he lived; as secretary to the lord proprietors of Carolina (1668–71), Secretary to the Council of Trade and Plantations (1673–74), and member of the Board of Trade (1696), Locke held key positions in bodies that oversaw the progress of Britain's colonization effort. He was employed, in short, to further the interests of the colonizers.

In Chapter 5, "Of Property," Locke contrasts those societies which, "with the use of money," have settled property arrangements among themselves, with those societies which have not done so:

> Yet there are still great tracts of ground to be found, which (the inhabitants thereof not having joined with the rest of mankind, in the consent of the use of their common money) lie waste, and are more than the people who dwell on it ... can make use of, and so still lie in common: though this can scarce happen among that part of mankind that have consented to the use of money.

Locke does not quite say in so many words that the right of the English colonizers in America to appropriate lands to themselves should be unrestricted so long as the "wild Indians" remained a society in which arrangements were not made using the currency of England. But that is surely the implication.

from Thomas Hobbes, *Leviathan* (1660)

from CHAPTER 13 "OF THE NATURAL CONDITION OF MANKIND AS CONCERNING THEIR FELICITY AND MISERY"

6. So that in the nature of man, we find three principal causes of quarrel. First, competition; secondly, diffidence;[1] thirdly, glory.

7. The first makes men invade for gain; the second, for safety; and the third, for reputation. The first use violence to make themselves masters of other men's persons, wives, children, and cattle; the second, to defend them; the third, for trifles, as a word, a smile, a different opinion, and any other sign of undervalue, either direct in their persons or by reflection in their kindred, their friends, their nation, their profession, or their name.

8. Hereby it is manifest that during the time men live without a common power to keep them all in awe,[2] they are in that condition which is called war; and such a war as is of every man against every

---

1   *diffidence*   Distrust.
2   *common power ... in awe*   I.e., a leader or government to keep them fearful of disobeying.

man. For War consists not in battle only, or the act of fighting, but in a tract[1] of time, wherein the will to contend by battle is sufficiently known; and therefore the notion of time is to be considered in the nature of war, as it is in the nature of weather. For as the nature of foul weather lies not in a shower or two of rain, but in an inclination thereto of many days together, so the nature of war consists not in actual fighting, but in the known disposition thereto during all the time there is no assurance to the contrary. All other time is Peace.

9. Whatsoever therefore is consequent to[2] a time of war, where every man is enemy to every man, the same consequent to the time wherein men live without other security than what their own strength and their own invention shall furnish them withal. In such condition there is no place for industry,[3] because the fruit thereof is uncertain; and consequently no culture[4] of the earth; no navigation, nor use of the commodities that may be imported by sea; no commodious building; no instruments of moving and removing such things as require much force; no knowledge of the face of the earth;[5] no account of time; no arts; no letters; no society; and which is worst of all, continual fear, and danger of violent death; and the life of man, solitary, poor, nasty, brutish, and short.

10. It may seem strange to some man that has not well weighed[6] these things that nature should thus dissociate and render men apt to invade and destroy one another; and he may therefore, not trusting to this inference, made from the passions, desire perhaps to have the same confirmed by experience. Let him therefore consider with himself; when taking a journey, he arms himself and seeks to go well accompanied; when going to sleep, he locks his doors; when even in his house he locks his chests; and this when he knows there be laws and public officers, armed to revenge all injuries shall be done him; what opinion he has of his fellow subjects, when he rides armed;

---

1   *tract*   Period.
2   *consequent to*   Results from.
3   *industry*   I.e., industriousness; productivity.
4   *culture*   Cultivation.
5   *knowledge of ... earth*   I.e., geographical knowledge.
6   *weighed*   Considered; thought about.

of his fellow citizens, when he locks his doors; and of his children, and servants, when he locks his chests. Does he not there as much accuse mankind by his actions as I do by my words? But neither of us accuse man's nature in it. The desires and other passions of man are in themselves no sin. No more are the actions that proceed from those passions till they know a law that forbids them; which, till laws be made, they cannot know; nor can any law be made till they have agreed upon the person that shall make it.

11. It may peradventure[1] be thought there was never such a time nor condition of war as this; and I believe it was never generally so, over all the world; but there are many places where they live so now. For the savage people in many places of America, except the government of small families, the concord whereof depends on natural lust, have no government at all, and live at this day in that brutish manner, as I said before. Howsoever, it may be perceived what manner of life there would be, where there were no common power to fear, by the manner of life which men that have formerly lived under a peaceful government use to degenerate into a civil war.

from John Locke, *The Second Treatise of Civil Government* (1689)

from CHAPTER 5
"OF PROPERTY"

Sec. 26. God, who has given the world to men in common, has also given them reason to make use of it to the best advantage of life and convenience. The earth, and all that is therein, is given to men for the support and comfort of their being. And though all the fruits it naturally produces, and beasts it feeds, belong to mankind in common as they are produced by the spontaneous hand of nature; and nobody has originally a private dominion, exclusive of[2] the rest of mankind, in any of them as they are thus in their natural state: yet being given for the use of men, there must of necessity be a means to appropriate[3] them some way or other, before they can be of any use,

---

1   *peradventure*   Perhaps.
2   *exclusive of*   Excluding.
3   *appropriate*   Come to own.

or at all beneficial to any particular man. The fruit, or venison, which nourishes the wild Indian, who knows no enclosure, and is still a tenant in common, must be his, and so his—i.e., a part of him—that another can no longer have any right to it, before it can do him any good for the support of his life.

Sec. 27. Though the earth, and all inferior creatures, be common to all men, yet every man has a property in his own person: this nobody has any right to but himself. The labor of his body, and the work of his hands, we may say, are properly his. Whatsoever then he removes out of the state that nature has provided, and left it in, he has mixed his labor with, and joined to it something that is his own, and thereby makes it his property. It being by him removed from the common state nature has placed it in, it has by this labor something annexed to it, that excludes the common right of other men: for this labor being the unquestionable property of the laborer, no man but he can have a right to what that is once joined to, at least where there is enough, and as good, left in common for others.

Sec. 28. He that is nourished by the acorns he picked up under an oak, or the apples he gathered from the trees in the wood, has certainly appropriated them to himself. Nobody can deny but the nourishment is his. I ask then, when did they begin to be his? When he digested? Or when he eat?[1] Or when he boiled? Or when he brought them home? Or when he picked them up? And it is plain, if the first gathering made them not his, nothing else could. That labor put a distinction between them and common: that added something to them more than nature, the common mother of all, had done; and so they became his private right. And will anyone say, he had no right to those acorns or apples he thus appropriated, because he had not the consent of all mankind to make them his? Was it a robbery thus to assume to himself what belonged to all in common? If such a consent as that was necessary, man had[2] starved, notwithstanding the plenty God had given him. We see in commons, which remain so by compact, that it is the taking any part of what is common, and removing it out of the state nature leaves it in, which begins the property; without which the common is of no use. And the taking of this or that

---

1   *eat* Ate.
2   *had* Would have.

part does not depend on the express consent of all the commoners.[1] Thus the grass my horse has bit, the turfs[2] my servant has cut, and the ore I have dug in any place, where I have a right to them in common with others, become my property, without the assignation or consent of anybody. The labor that was mine, removing them out of that common state they were in, has fixed my property in them. ...

Sec. 30. Thus this law of reason makes the deer that Indian's who has killed it; it is allowed to be his goods, who has bestowed his labor upon it, though before it was the common right of everyone. And among those who are counted the civilized part of mankind, who have made and multiplied positive[3] laws to determine property, this original law of nature, for the beginning of property, in what was before common, still takes place; and by virtue thereof, what fish anyone catches in the ocean, that great and still remaining common of mankind; or what ambergris[4] anyone takes up here, is by the labor that removes it out of that common state nature left it in, made his property who takes that pains about it. And even among us, the hare that anyone is hunting, is thought his who pursues her during the chase: for being a beast that is still looked upon as common, and no man's private possession, whoever has employed so much labor about any of that kind, as to find and pursue her, has thereby removed her from the state of nature, wherein she was common, and has begun a property. ...

Sec. 32. But the chief matter of property being now not the fruits of the earth and the beasts that subsist on it, but the earth itself, as that which takes in and carries with it all the rest, I think it is plain, that property in that too is acquired as the former. As much land as a man tills, plants, improves, cultivates, and can use the product of, so much is his property. He by his labor does, as it were, enclose it from the common. Nor will it invalidate his right to say everybody else has an equal title to it; and therefore he cannot appropriate, he cannot enclose, without the consent of all his fellow-commoners, all mankind. God, when he gave the world in common to all mankind,

---

1   *commoners* Those who own the land in common.
2   *turfs* Slabs of peat, used as fuel.
3   *positive* Formally enacted.
4   *ambergris* Waxy substance secreted by sperm whales, used in making perfume. It is found on beaches or floating on the ocean.

commanded man also to labor, and the penury[1] of his condition required it of him. God and his reason commanded him to subdue the earth, i.e., improve it for the benefit of life, and therein lay out something upon it that was his own, his labor. He that in obedience to this command of God subdued, tilled and sowed any part of it, thereby annexed to it something that was his property, which another had no title to, nor could without injury take from him. ...

Sec. 34. God gave the world to men in common; but since he gave it them for their benefit, and the greatest conveniences of life they were capable to draw from it, it cannot be supposed he meant it should always remain common and uncultivated. He gave it to the use of the industrious and rational (and labor was to be his title to it), not to the fancy or covetousness of the quarrelsome and contentious. He that had as good left for his improvement, as was already taken up, needed not complain, ought not to meddle with what was already improved by another's labor: if he did, it is plain he desired the benefit of another's pains, which he had no right to, and not the ground which God had given him in common with others to labor on, and whereof there was as good left, as that already possessed, and more than he knew what to do with, or his industry could reach to. ...

Sec. 36. The measure of property nature has well set by the extent of men's labor and the conveniences of life. No man's labor could subdue, or appropriate all; nor could his enjoyment consume more than a small part; so that it was impossible for any man, this way, to entrench[2] upon the right of another, or acquire to himself a property to the prejudice[3] of his neighbor, who would still have room for as good and as large a possession (after the other had taken out his) as before it was appropriated. This measure did confine every man's possession to a very moderate proportion, and such as he might appropriate to himself without injury to anybody, in the first ages of the world, when men were more in danger to be lost, by wandering from their company, in the then-vast wilderness of the earth, than to be straitened[4] for want of room to plant in. And the same measure may be allowed still without prejudice to anybody, as full as the world

---

1 *penury* Poverty.
2 *entrench* Trespass.
3 *prejudice* Disadvantage.
4 *straitened* Restricted.

seems: for supposing a man, or family, in the state they were at first peopling of the world by the children of Adam or Noah; let him plant in some inland, vacant places of America, we shall find that the possessions he could make himself, upon the measures we have given, would not be very large, nor, even to this day, prejudice the rest of mankind, or give them reason to complain, or think themselves injured by this man's encroachment, though the race of men have now spread themselves to all the corners of the world, and do infinitely exceed the small number was at the beginning. Nay, the extent of ground is of so little value, without labor, that I have heard it affirmed that in Spain itself a man may be permitted to plough, sow and reap, without being disturbed, upon land he has no other title to, but only his making use of it. But, on the contrary, the inhabitants think themselves beholden to him who, by his industry on neglected, and consequently waste land, has increased the stock of corn[1] which they wanted. But be this as it will, which I lay no stress on; this I dare boldly affirm, that the same rule of propriety, *viz.*,[2] that every man should have as much as he could make use of, would hold still in the world, without straitening anybody; since there is land enough in the world to suffice double the inhabitants, had not the invention of money, and the tacit agreement of men to put a value on it, introduced (by consent) larger possessions, and a right to them; which, how it has done, I shall by and by show more at large.

Sec. 37. This is certain, that in the beginning, before the desire of having more than man needed had altered the intrinsic value of things, which depends only on their usefulness to the life of man; or had agreed, that a little piece of yellow metal, which would keep without wasting or decay, should be worth a great piece of flesh,[3] or a whole heap of corn; though men had a right to appropriate, by their labor, each one of himself, as much of the things of nature as he could use: yet this could not be much, nor to the prejudice of others, where the same plenty was still left to those who would use the same industry. To which let me add, that he who appropriates land to himself by his labor, does not lessen, but increase the common stock of mankind: for the provisions serving to the support of human life,

---

1   *corn*   Grain.
2   *viz.*   Abbreviation of the Latin videlicet, meaning "namely," or "that is to say."
3   *flesh*   Meat.

produced by one acre of enclosed and cultivated land, are (to speak much within compass[1]) ten times more than those which are yielded by an acre of land of an equal richness lying waste in common. And therefore he that encloses land, and has a greater plenty of the conveniences of life from ten acres than he could have from an hundred left to nature, may truly be said to give ninety acres to mankind; for his labor now supplies him with provisions out of ten acres, which were but the product of an hundred lying in common. I have here rated the improved land very low, in making its product but as ten to one, when it is much nearer an hundred to one: for I ask, whether in the wild woods and uncultivated waste of America, left to nature, without any improvement, tillage or husbandry,[2] a thousand acres yield the needy and wretched inhabitants as many conveniences of life, as ten acres of equally fertile land do in Devonshire, where they are well cultivated? ...

Sec. 41. There cannot be a clearer demonstration of anything, than several nations of the Americans are of this, who are rich in land, and poor in all the comforts of life; whom nature having furnished as liberally as any other people, with the materials of plenty, i.e., a fruitful soil, apt to produce in abundance, what might serve for food, raiment,[3] and delight; yet for want of improving it by labor, have not one hundredth part of the conveniences we enjoy; and a king of a large and fruitful territory there, feeds, lodges, and is clad worse than a day-laborer in England. ...

Sec. 43. An acre of land, that bears here twenty bushels of wheat, and another in America, which, with the same husbandry, would do the like, are, without doubt, of the same natural intrinsic value: but yet the benefit mankind receives from the one in a year, is worth five pounds and from the other possibly not worth a penny, if all the profit an Indian received from it were to be valued, and sold here; at least, I may truly say, not one thousandth. It is labor then which puts the greatest part of value upon land, without which it would scarcely be worth anything. It is to that we owe the greatest part of all its useful products; for all that the straw, bran, bread, of that acre of wheat, is more worth than the product of an acre of as good

---

1   *to speak ... within compass*   To speak carefully, avoiding exaggeration.
2   *husbandry*   Agriculture.
3   *raiment*   Clothing.

land, which lies waste, is all the effect of labor; for it is not barely the ploughman's pains, the reaper's and thresher's toil, and the baker's sweat, [that] is to be counted into the bread we eat; the labor of those who broke the oxen, who dug and wrought the iron and stones, who felled and framed the timber employed about the plough, mill, oven, or any other utensils, which are a vast number, requisite to this corn, from its being feed to be sown to its being made bread, must all be charged on the account of labor, and received as an effect of that. Nature and the earth furnished only the almost worthless materials, as in themselves. It would be a strange catalogue of things, that industry provided and made use of, about every loaf of bread, before it came to our use, if we could trace them; iron, wood, leather, bark, timber, stone, bricks, coals, lime, cloth, dyeing drugs,[1] pitch, tar, masts, ropes, and all the materials made use of in the ship, that brought any of the commodities made use of by any of the workmen, to any part of the work; all which it would be almost impossible, at least too long, to reckon up. ...

Sec. 49. Thus in the beginning all the world was America, and more so than that is now; for no such thing as money was anywhere known. Find out something that has the use and value of money among his neighbors, you shall see the same man will begin presently to enlarge his possessions.

from George Washington, letter to James Duane,[2] 7 September 1783

Rocky Hill

Sir,

I have carefully perused the papers which you put into my hands relating to Indian Affairs. ...

My ideas therefore of the line of conduct proper to be observed not only towards the Indians, but for the government of the citizens of America, in their settlement of the western country (which is intimately connected therewith) are simply these. ...

---

1 *dyeing drugs* Substances for dyeing cloth.
2 *James Duane* American Revolutionary leader and later mayor of New York City (1733–97).

That the Indians could be informed, that after a contest of eight years for sovereignty of the country,[1] G[reat] Britain has ceded all the lands of the United States within the limits described by the … Provisional Treaty.

That as they (the Indians), maugre[2] all the advice and admonition which could be given them at the commencement and during the prosecution of the war, could not be restrained from acts of hostility, but were determined to join their arms to those of G[reat] Britain and to share their fortune; so, consequently, with a less generous people than Americans, they would be made to share the same fate, and be compelled to retire along with them beyond the Lakes.[3] But as we prefer peace to a state of warfare, as we consider them as a deluded people, as we persuade ourselves that they are convinced, from experience, of their error in taking up the hatchet against us, and that their true interest and safety must now depend upon *our* friendship. As the country is large enough to contain us all, and as we are disposed to be kind to them and to partake of their trade, we will from these considerations and from motives of comp[anionship], draw a veil over what is past and establish a boundary line between them and us beyond which we will *endeavor* to restrain our people from hunting or settling, and within which they shall not come, but for the purposes of trading, treating, or other business unexceptionable in its nature.

In establishing this line, in the first instance, care should be taken neither to yield nor to grasp at too much. But to endeavor to impress the Indians with an idea of the generosity of our disposition to accommodate them, and with the necessity we are under, of providing for our warriors, our young people who are growing up, and strangers who are coming from other countries to live among us. And if they should make a point of it, or appear dissatisfied at the line we may find it necessary to establish, compensation should be made them for their claims within it. …

… [T]he settlement of the western country and making a peace with the Indians are so analogous that there can be no definition of

---

1 *contest … the country* I.e., the Revolutionary War. Many Indigenous groups fought on the British side during this conflict, predicting that a unified and independent America would introduce further threats to their land.
2 *maugre* Despite.
3 *the Lakes* I.e., the Great Lakes.

the one without involving considerations of the other. For I repeat it, again, and I am clear in my opinion, that policy and economy point very strongly to the expediency of being upon good terms with the Indians, and the propriety of purchasing their lands in preference to attempting to drive them by force of arms out of their country; which as we have already experienced is like driving the wild beasts of the forest which will return as soon as the pursuit is at an end and fall perhaps on those that are left there; when the gradual extension of our settlements will as certainly cause the savage as the wolf to retire; both being beasts of prey though they differ in shape. In a word there is nothing to be obtained by an Indian war but the soil they live on, and this can be had by purchase at less expense, and without that bloodshed and those distresses which helpless women and children are made partakers of in all kinds of disputes with them.

If there is anything in these thoughts (which I have fully and freely communicated) worthy [of] attention I shall be happy and am, Sir,

Your most obedient servant,

G[eorge] Washington

From the Publisher

A name never says it all, but the word "Broadview"
expresses a good deal of the philosophy behind our
company. We are open to a broad range of academic
approaches and political viewpoints. We pay attention to the broad impact book publishing and book
printing has in the wider world; for some years now
we have used 100% recycled paper for most titles.
Our publishing program is internationally oriented
and broad-ranging. Our individual titles often appeal
to a broad readership too; many are of interest as
much to general readers as to academics and students.

Founded in 1985, Broadview remains a fully independent company owned by its shareholders—not an
imprint or subsidiary of a larger multinational.

To order our books or obtain up-to-date
information, please visit
broadviewpress.com.

broadview press
www.broadviewpress.com

This book is made of paper from well-managed FSC® - certified forests, recycled materials, and other controlled sources.